MW01243229

Mike Albanese's

The Werewolf's Apprentice

Copyright © 2018 Mike Albanese

The Werewolf's Apprentice

Thanks to.

Dorothy Chandler - Editor

Cover by Susan Gerardi

Thanks to those who helped along the way.

Joanne Poyourow, Lara Sterling, Leslie House, Debee Stayner, David Gaz.

And the ever patient and forgiving.

Virginia and Joey Albanese

The Werewolf's Apprentice

"*But those that seek my soul, to destroy it, shall go into the lower parts of the earth... They shall fall by the sword, they shall be apportioned for foxes.*"

— Psalms 63

The Werewolf's Apprentice

The House on Sawmill Road

THE OLD MAN stood behind a band of yellow police tape watching the house burn.

A cop nearby was talking to a fireman about last night's football game. The rest of the crew showed no sign of urgency. They shuffled around knocking down spot fires on the lawn. The roof gave way, blowing sparks high into the air leaving behind the glowing stump of a brick chimney.

"How many inside?" The cop asked.

"Three, two adults and a teen age boy," said the fireman.

"Three? One's missing, there were two boys," said the cop. He scanned the line of trees behind the house.

"What we gonna do about that?" the fireman asked. "I ain't going in those woods after him."

"He won't get far. We'll bring in Decker and his dogs."

The Werewolf's Apprentice

The fireman handed the cop three evidence bags with ears in them. "Fifteen thousand, not bad for a night's work."

"Here comes the press, get in character." He rubbed his cheek and forehead with soot.

Leon watched the men from the edge of the woods. He was chasing deer when the men in the trucks arrived. Big men in black trucks with DEA on the sides. They surrounded his house with lights, his father came to the door and they shot him. The men stepped over his father's body. Leon jumped as he heard more shots, he knew they were all dead. The men dragged his father's body into the house. More men carried boxes into the house. Moments after they stepped away, the house exploded and caught fire. Only after the fire had established itself beyond control did the red trucks arrive. They made a big show of unloading hoses, shouting and playing heroes to the crowd.

The Werewolf's Apprentice

With the house fully lit, the firemen turned to soaking the adjoining houses and chasing down sparks headed for the woods nearby.

The boy remained hidden, holding back. His wolf blood burned. He longed for one of the men to come into the forest, he ached to taste blood and feel the death struggle in his jaws. He could take them. He could take them all. He pushed down hard on his rising wolf side, if he started, one dead fireman would never be enough.

The old man walked from the crowd into the forest. Out of sight, he took off his clothes and shifted. Now the werewolf, he took in the smell and sounds of the fire and the men talking. He knew the family, he knew the boy was still alive. He trotted along the perimeter of the tree line scenting for the child. He found the boy. The boy had shifted, the old man saw clear yellow eyes lying in wait, a wild thing ready to fight for its life. The wolf-child rose, hundred year eyes met new eyes. The old wolf sighed at this new obligation.

"Bone?" the boy asked.

"Come with me. There isn't much time."

They trotted at speed across the forest floor. Bone ran faster than his age, he knew the trails. The younger wolf ran close behind. They crawled under the strands of barbed wire at the edge of a black tar road.

"Piss here at the edge of the road." Bone said. "Dogs will be coming soon." The boy lifted his leg. The old wolf watched. "Don't step in it. We shift back now and run through that ditch to that trailer up there, the water will hide our scent. The dogs will prefer your wolf sign. Let's get moving."

The old man led the boy up the ditch to a salmon colored singlewide with dirty gray awnings set behind a chain link fence. He went to a shed and returned with an insect sprayer, he pumped it up and sprayed the water in the ditch, he soaked down the path from the road to the trailer.

"Deet, wrecks the dog's noses," he told the boy. "Everybody uses it out here for bugs, they won't suspect."

The old man stood high and retrieved a key from a rafter and opened the door. Inside he pulled two bathrobes from the closet, he handed one to the boy.

Bone went to the refrigerator and gave Leon a rare porterhouse steak. The kid tore into it.

"Why'd you cook this thing? It tastes funny," Leon said.

"Lasts longer. I don't go out much these days."

Bone turned on the TV news. The boy stared at the image of the burning house.

A reporter questioned a man wearing a satin bomber jacket with a gold badge pinned on it.

"What happened?" he asked.

The Werewolf's Apprentice

"Drug raid, this house was being used to manufacture methamphetamine. The officers entered the house, were met by gunfire. They were forced to shoot the occupants. Evidently the chemicals set off an explosion, hence the rapid fire."

"And the occupants?" the reporter asked.

The fireman spoke, "Three dead, one adult male, one adult female and one younger boy around fifteen. We were unable to recover the bodies."

"Who are those men?" asked the boy.

"'Animal Control,' werewolf hunters. They're back again. The guy in the satin jacket is Daniel Patrick. He's the boss."

"He's lying," the boy said.

"Yes, he is," said Bone.

Officer Jim Decker arrived at the house in his dog truck. He stepped out in a blue jump suit with *Decker* written in gold script across the back. He had a gleaming hand tooled leather gun belt hanging on low on his hip. A pearl handled Ruger rode high in the holster at his hand. Decker stood at the cage with his bloodhounds. A cop held out a shoe.

"You sure this is his?"

"Yeah, we got it from his room."

Decker shook a Marlboro Red from a flip top box and lit it with a silver monogrammed lighter. "It's cold and lonely out there. He's scared. Might hurt himself. My dogs will take care of him."

Decker whispered to his dogs as he passed the shoe under their noses. The lead dog lost his mind with joy, he bayed and took off. Decker and two deputies ran behind following the dog's collar via GPS. They found the boy's clothes. The hounds jumped on the wolf scent and took off through the woods.

The Werewolf's Apprentice

The sound of the hunt came in through the trailer window. Bone stood in the door listening. He sat down next to the boy. There was no fear in his voice, "Here they come."

"Will they find me?"

"Maybe, probably not. Nothing is for certain, but our odds are good. Those dogs can't stand the Deet. These cops are in a hurry, they won't spend much time on an old man. Don't touch the lights. Go in the back and shower. Wash all that woods smell off you. Don't forget the hair. There's a bottle of Deet in there. Rub it all over you, everywhere, you got me? Everywhere. It's gonna burn a bit down there. Get down on the floor between the bed and the wall farthest from the door, lay there like a corpse. Go, do it quick."

Bone opened the door, sprayed Deet around the top and sides of the door. He thought of the Passover Bible story. He grinned and muttered something in Latin about deliverance from evil as he made the sign of the cross with

The Werewolf's Apprentice

the spray wand. Bone shot a final stream down the hall. He went to the porch and sat in the dark holding a quart of malt liquor and a cigar.

A hound's floppy ears got caught in the barbed wire. Decker cut the fence with metal snips he carried. The dogs ran to the road and milled around crying and scratching at the dark stain.

"The trail stops here. Somebody picked him up."

"Lucky timing," the deputy said.

"Lucky my ass, another shifter I bet," said Decker. "These woods are full of them."

He looked up the road.

"There's a trailer over that way. Let's go take a look."

The three men and the dogs arrived at Bone's trailer. Bone shuffled to meet them in a pair of ragged fleece lined bed slippers holding his bottle and cigar. He stood unsteady, holding himself up against the gate.

The Werewolf's Apprentice

"Good evening officers. Is there something I can help you with?"

Decker profiled Bone; another stubble faced trailer park geezer, living on cigarettes and cheap beer with a social security check to cover the rent.

"Do you have an id?" Decker asked.

"My friends call me Bone. I got my license and my social card in the house somewheres. You want me to go find it?"

"That won't be necessary Bone. We're looking for a boy, fifteen or so. His parents reported him missing. Have you seen anything? A truck or car that might have picked him up?"

"Been out here all afternoon. Not much traffic, we off the main road, a Camry drove by here a while ago. I used to have a Camry you know. When I was younger I'd drive nothing but a Camry."

"I like Camry's too, what about that car?"

The Werewolf's Apprentice

"Stopped down there a ways an' kept going."

"What color?"

"Hard to tell. White, I guess, nothing special, just a Camry. I sold my Camry to this guy from Knoxville. Gave me sixteen hundred dollars for it. The tires weren't so good but he gave me all the money anyway. Now I got this El Camino over there. It broke down a while back, I can't pay to get it fixed."

Decker looked Bone in the eyes. "Bone, the car, did you see anyone?"

"I can't see so good, they made me take that test at the motor department last year. They said I need glasses. I went to the VA in Knoxville but they told me I needed government papers. I got no government papers. Just my social card."

"Did you see the license plate? On the car?"

"I saw it, but that light was burned out like on the Camry like I had. They gave me a ticket for that. Cost thirty

13

dollars. My brother says a Camry is a piece of shit. But he never had one so what would he know? I had this Thunderbird once, nineteen seventy-seven with them velour seats. It had an AC that could freeze the tits off a bullfrog. I drove that car for years. What kind of cars you police drive these days? You still drive them Crown Vics?"

"They don't make them anymore, we drive Ford Escapes now. Can we get back to the boy? Did you see a boy?"

"I was kinda sleepy. I drink the malt almost every night to calm my nerves. I was in the 'Nam, I went to the VA for that PSTD test, they said I needed a VA card, I got no VA card. They told me to go to the county clinic. I don't need no VA doctors, malt just as good for the PSTD.

Bone yawned and blew out blended wave of beer and cigar stink in Decker's direction. He put the dead cigar in his mouth and scratched his stomach through the buttons of his shirt.

14

The Werewolf's Apprentice

The dog truck arrived.

Decker handed Bone his card. "If the kid shows up, give us a call. Try to keep him around until we get here."

"Yessir officer. You can count on Bone, I'll be looking for him."

The truck left with Decker and his hounds. Bone sat head down on the bench for another hour with his mouth hanging open, watching the road. He went into the trailer and turned off all the lights. In the bedroom he looked at the still form of the boy.

"Is it ok?"

"They're gone. For now."

The Next Day

Leon woke to find his spindly fifteen year old legs tangled in Bone's huge bathrobe. He went to the kitchen, on the refrigerator was a note. "Back soon. Don't go outside." Leon drank from the tap and turned on the television. He flipped through the channels looking for news. The local station was running a story about the terrible condition of the local school bus fleet. He turned down the sound.

Leon jumped to the sound of tires on the gravel outside. Bone pushed the door open with his foot and dumped plastic bags on the floor. He placed a box hair dye on the kitchen counter.

"Come on over here, we gonna make you beautiful."

Bone went to work with the dye, turning Leon's shiny black hair into a light frizzy blonde.

The Werewolf's Apprentice

"Guess I went too far, looks like I cooked your hair," he said. "No matter, I can fix that."

Bone rattled around in the drawer an came up with an old Sunbeam clipper. He set it on three and reduced Leon's head to a hairy yellow cue ball.

"You look like a local now boy. Don't go shifting on me I don't wanna do this again."

"I got you some clothes at the thrift shop over there, I guessed at the size, we can get more later, still need some shoes, I got some flip flops you can wear for now." He went to the kitchen and stuffed the microwave with bacon.

"Bone," the boy said.

"Yes, Leon."

"Why do they hunt us?"

"Fear mostly, the struggle goes back centuries. They fear of what they cannot control. But you are something new, you are what they fear most, the wolf-child, the hybrid shifter. Half human, half werewolf. They're scared shitless you might start breeding more of your kind. Us old guys are a little scared of you as well if you must know the truth."

"It smells funny in here. What's in those bags in the bedroom?"

"It's a werewolf rule. The trash guys look for cans full of bacon wrappers and meat trays, ice cream buckets. Tell the cops. What you put in the can outside and what goes in the bags is rule number one. I take the bags to that truck stop down the interstate. Use places where they cook a lot, like steak houses, never a fast food place, too many cameras."

"I guess there are lots of rules," said the boy. "Mom and dad had rules too."

"We leave tonight."

"I got nothing left here," said the boy.

They sat at the coffee table watching the silent TV eating bacon and ice cream.

The Werewolf's Apprentice

"How did they find us?" Leon asked.

"Some little thing, it's always that way. A piece of the truth leaks out. Like having nothing but meat and ice cream in the refrigerator. Mistaking a silver fork for a chrome one at a friend's house. Full moon problems. Lots of ways to trip up. It's best to keep moving."

"Mom and dad never talked about where they met or about us living out west."

"If you don't know you can't screw things up."

Bone looked at the boy. "It would happen this way. You mention a place where you lived to some kid at school. One day you're at his birthday party, his father asks you what Bisbee Arizona was like. Dad's a cop. He's watching your face. You don't have to say a thing, he reads your face. Now he's got you."

"I saw that man on TV, I looked up the story on the internet, he's a Knoxville detective."

The Werewolf's Apprentice

"His name is Turner, he or that Patrick guy found out something, about your mother probably, she goes way back."

"But what did they do? They never hurt anyone. Why?"

"It's a complicated story, only one of us needs to know right now."

"Last night, those men with the dogs. They won't stop, will they?"

"No, they won't. They'll be back, more questions, more traps to fall into. That's why we have to leave."

Bone opened the thrift shop bag and dumped the clothes on the couch. Leon started on the second hand jeans with the scissors, cutting off buttons and zippers. He could smell the bodies that used to wear them. He sewed on Velcro strips to hold the waist together, he razored slits in the elastic of the underwear. The shoes he will buy won't have laces, never laces, only elastic bands that will part when he shifts.

The Werewolf's Apprentice

Bone came from the back room carrying an alligator brief case. "This is for you, your father told me to give it to you if anything happened."

"What's in it? It must be important."

"Never looked, not my business."

"Dad made me learn a number, 549, he told me to never forget it."

"Here, try it on this." Bone placed the case on Leon's lap.

Leon rolled in the combination and raised the lid. "What's all this?"

"Must be two hundred thousand in there. That's a shitload of money," Bone said. "What's in that leather bag?"

"It's heavy," the boy said.

Leon pulled out a 357 magnum revolver. Loose in another bag were bullets. Leon picked one up. "Ouch, it burns."

"That's odd." Bone took one by the brass case and rubbed it on his pants leg.

"These points are silver. Werewolf loads. You can't buy these, your father had to make them."

"Why would dad have a gun with silver bullets?"

Bone held the poison metal to his face, "Your mother had some interesting friends."

Bone rummaged through the case. He found a picture and gave it to Leon. It was a photo of his parents standing in front of a black and white car with a ram's head and the letters HEMI on the hood.

"They look so young," said Leon.

Bone ran his fingers along the inside of the case. He found a blue band attached to a wolf's head. "This belonged to your mother. I don't see anything else, seems he would have left you a message or something."

Leon turned the weapon over in his hands. "This is the message."

The Werewolf's Apprentice

Bone touched his rough fingers to the boy's hand, "Listen to me, those men want you to come after them, full of rage, unskilled and angry. They're counting on it. Deny them that advantage. Let them live... for now. Let them sleep comfortable in their beds, be patient, they will be yours soon enough. There aren't many of us left in this world. Revenge can wait, our first duty is to survive."

"When do we go?"

"Tonight."

"Where?"

"South Dakota, we have people out there that can help us."

"Will the El Camino make it?"

"Maybe, those tags are flagged by now. We'll fly. No cops, no gas station cameras, no questions."

"I don't have an id."

"These people won't ask for one."

The Werewolf's Apprentice

Wereskeetos

They drove north up I-75 and took Tennessee forty-one to the lake country. Bone turned onto a clay road that ended at a run-down fish camp on the shore of Norris lake. He rubbed Deet over his arms, face and neck. He passed the bottle to the boy.

"They have mosquitoes here the size of bumble bees," he said. "We don't want to start some kind of wereskeeto infestation."

"Wereskeetos, never thought of that."

Bone's lined face smiled, "That would be a real mess."

He parked the El Camino on the boat ramp.

"What are we doing here?"

Bone smiled and lit a Camel. "You'll see."

He and the boy sat at the end of the dock, watching fish jump at fireflies.

The Werewolf's Apprentice

A half hour passed in the dark, there was no moon. The air smelled of rotting plants. Stars reflected off the mirror of the lake.

Off in the distance came the sound of engines in the sky. Bone went to the El Camino and turned on the lights.

The seaplane came in low like a great black bird painting wind ripples on the lake. It circled over the far end and dropped, cutting lines into water. It was an ancient twin-engine Grumman Goose, no markings or lights of any kind. It idled up to the dock. The engines went silent. All they could hear were frogs and the plane's wake hissing into the shore. A man stuck his head out of the cargo hatch and tossed Bone a rope.

"Right on time," said Bone.

"At your service." He embraced Bone. "Good to see you again, old friend."

"We're glad to see you."

The Werewolf's Apprentice

Leon focused on the stranger, he looked like a dope runner, aviator sunglasses hanging around his neck with kakis crumpled down around a ratty pair of black tennis shoes. The outline of a pistol showed through the back pocket of his pants.

"Is this the customer?"

"Leon, this is Parker, Parker meet Leon. I'm coming too," said Bone, "I'm out of time here."

Parker shook Leon's hand, it was rough, another stranger in Leon's tattered life. Leon looked for clues in the man's face, he saw a measure of quiet determination, not unlike Bone. Who were these men? So many changes, so many faces, so fast. All he wanted was a chance to breathe, touch something familiar.

Bone went to the El Camino, rolled down the windows, released the brake and stood by as it eased down the ramp into the lake. It floated out a ways and went to the bottom.

"Really liked that car."

The Werewolf's Apprentice

Leon sat in the co-pilot seat under the yellow glow of the instruments watching Parker's every move. The plane smelled of cigarettes and motor oil.

Parker set the magnetos to *run*, started the engines and moved the throttles to idle. The plane eased away from the dock on a line to the most distant shore. Parker pushed the throttles to full power, Leon felt the gravity of acceleration in his seat. After a short run the plane cleared the water and banked to the west. Parker flew low and fast along the contours of the valleys skimming the pines. He slid back the plexiglass vent. Bone's cigarette smoke floated through the cockpit and out into the night.

"We fly fast and low, at the treetops where their radar can't see us." Parker said.

Leon looked for the lights of Knoxville, but they were long gone along with high school friends, drive in hamburgers and his first kiss. He saw in his mind the smoldering wreck of his home and the faces of the laughing men that destroyed his world. His young heart hardened against them. His anger became a weight against his youth. He wiped his eyes and settled in his seat, looking through the water stained glass onto a broader world.

Faith

Bone shook him awake.

"Wake up kid, time to go to work."

Leon looked out the window, the hills were gone, replaced by long empty brown fields.

"Where are we?"

"Idaho, low on fuel."

"What do we do?"

Bone motioned him to the back of the plane where two large drums were lashed to the floor. Bone lay out a hose and clipped into a fitting near the wing. He pointed to a hand crank pump on one of the drums. "Start cranking, you take the first shift, we got over three hundred gallons here, it's gonna take a while."

Leon worked the crank until his arms turned to rubber. Bone watched him from the cockpit while he talked to Parker.

The Werewolf's Apprentice

"Had enough?" Bone asked.

"Just getting going." Leon said.

Bone came back and took the handle. "You don't have to prove anything today. The right is tank full, swing that red valve over there to the left, I'll take the other one."

Bone finished off the second barrel. Parker slowed and circled over a small lake. Bone took an axe and hacked holes in the sides of the drums.

Bone slid the cargo bay open. "These gotta go, gotta lighten the ship, can't leave a trail. One hand for the strap, one hand for the barrel. Let's go."

Leon held back from the wind roaring through the gaping door and the sight of water a hundred feet below him.

Bone's voice was stern, "Get over here Leon."

They pushed out the drums and slid the cargo door closed. Leon was shaking.

The Werewolf's Apprentice

Parker smiled at Leon. "Thanks for the gas. Wanna fly the Goose?"

"Oh yeah."

Parker dropped the Goose into the lake and killed the motors.

"Parker you are an asshole," Bone said. "We could have fell out back there."

Parker motioned Leon forward "Let's get started."

He led him through the switches and knobs.

"That one," Parker pointed, "press it hard." Leon held the big red toggle switch up against *Start*, the engines turned over and ignited blowing blue oil smoke across the water.

"Take the wheel, hold it steady, I'll work the throttles. Do exactly what I say, and do it smooth, no jerking."

Leon grasped the control, the grease stained leather was heaven in his hands.

The Werewolf's Apprentice

Parker jammed the engines wide open, the Grumman surged forward. Leon held the wheel so tight he thought his fingers would break. The plane waddled forward in the waves at first then rose until it planed like a jet ski, the wings began to lift.

"Steady, steady, almost there." Parker caught Leon flashing a look. Parker leaned back in his seat looking out the window with his arms crossed. Leon broke out in a sweat. "Yup sonny boy, it's all on you now. Pull back slow until we get some air, let the plane do the work."

The patient and forgiving Goose cleared the water and relaxed, it gently floated higher. A stand of oak trees on the shore came on fast, filling up the window like a green wall. Leon froze.

"That's good for a start," Parker took the controls. Leon smiled until his face hurt.

Hours later they crossed the Cheyenne River, Parker scrubbed off speed and cranked down the wheels. Soon the

The Werewolf's Apprentice

Goose was on the ground at the one lane airport that served Faith, South Dakota. Two men met the plane with a forklift and pulled it into a hangar. The high metal doors closed behind. Inside the hanger were two more Goose. One had been stripped for parts.

Waiting for the passengers was a gentle looking man of some stature and quiet intelligence, mid-thirties or so and a woman. She looked strong in her rough shirt, jeans and brown cowboy boots.

"Are they shifters?" Leon whispered to Bone.

"They ALL are shifters. We're home."

"Leon, this is Tony and Maureen. They'll be looking after you for a while."

"I thought we'd be together." Leon said.

"I'm not going anywhere, you need a proper home. I'm not that guy."

"School?"

Maureen spoke, "Yes, we have a school. You might like it a bit better than your last one."

"I don't want it."

Parker stared Leon into silence. "What's a knot Leon?"

"That's a dumb question."

"The Goose cruises at one hundred seventy-five knots. What's a that in miles per hour?"

"I don't know."

"Two hundred one. When you can do that math in your head come to me and we'll see if we can make a pilot out of you. No more chasing deer in the woods. This is the real world. Grow up, learn something useful and never forget who your friends are."

Maureen led the reluctant Leon to her stretch cab pickup. Leon got in the back. Next to him was a lean teenage girl in jeans and a hoodie, she had shifter eyes, black movie star hair and perfect lips, she looked fifteen.

Leon had never seen anything like her. She pulled her messenger bag over to make room.

"Leon, this is Samantha, she's new here, just like you, came in last week."

Samantha looked Leon over. He felt simple and uncomfortable with his dirty hands and baggy thrift shop clothes.

"Nice to meet you Leon. What happened to your hair?"

"Bone did that. It'll grow out. Long trip, I'm glad to be here," he said.

"It's a good place."

"Where are you from?" he asked.

Samantha looked down at her shoes, she bit the tip of her thumb.

Maureen caught Leon's eye in the rear view. "We don't ask that around here Leon."

"I'm sorry. Is that one of the rules?"

"No, we just don't do it."

"I'm from Charleston." Samantha said.

"Knoxville."

"Did you come alone?"

Leon's voice tripped on his words, "Yes, Bone brought me in."

"Me too," she said.

With that she pulled her bag up to her chest and turned to the window. Leon didn't ask for more.

* * * * *

Three days on, a man fishing for bass at Norris lake caught the prop of his outboard motor on the El Camino. Suspecting a stolen car or worse he called the state police. Decker the dog guy and his boss, Turner, showed up too. They all stood watching as the car was winched out of the lake.

The Werewolf's Apprentice

"Crafty old bastard," said Decker, "Malt liquor geezer drunk with bad breath, my Camry this, my Camry that. PSTD. He played me good."

Turner took a picture of the license tag with his phone. "The boy got away, you said you'd take care of him."

Decker ran his tongue over his lips. "Just another baby shifter, small fry, careless, stupid. This one's no different. I'll get him."

Turner looked at his watch, "That boy's not gonna forget about you."

The Werewolf's Apprentice

Wisconsin Five Years On

It was the first anniversary of Leon and Samantha's running pickup missions. Animal Control was at full strength, deploying all the tools of the human state against the shifters. Map pins on a wall in Virginia tallied the score, the shifters were losing badly.

In the pitch dark cockpit of a 1939 Grumman Goose Leon rapped a sticky oil gauge with his knuckle. It didn't move. He and Samantha sat looking out the windows, listening to waves lap against the thin aluminum skin of the seaplane.

"Where are they?" She poked her head out the escape hatch. The cold night air flooded into the cockpit. She scanned the shoreline of the icy Wisconsin lake with night vision binoculars. "Damn this fog, I can't see a thing. They should be here by now."

The Werewolf's Apprentice

Leon bent over the racing numbers of the police scanner as it squawked traffic calls and chit chat from the patrol cars on the interstate.

"Over there, I see the boat," she said. "A light just flashed three-two-three."

"Finally," Leon ran through the check list and unlatched the start buttons for the engines. "I'll go back for the customers."

Samantha took Leon's place in the pilot's seat. She was now a tall young woman, on the trailing edge of twenty with a face older than her years. The lights of the console reflected off her unnaturally blue eyes, a wolf's head hung from her neck on a blue silk band.

An aluminum skiff running dark emerged from the cold fog towards the plane. Leon opened the cargo door and caught the line from the boat.

A woman in the front stretched a baby out to Leon across the water. The child was wrapped in a silver thermal

The Werewolf's Apprentice

blanket. In his arms Leon met a set of trusting metallic eyes shot with yellow streaks.

The eyes, always the eyes.

He passed the child to Samantha and helped the others inside. The man at the outboard waved and turned back.

Leon surveyed the passengers. The mother was thirty or so, there were raw thorn scratches on her face. She was wearing an expensive down ski jacket. Her hair was full of leaves, she looked like hell. Next to her was a man, possibly the father. He had the face of a hunted thing. Two young boys made up the rest. They were excited, looking around the cabin, feeling the adventure, unaware of the possibilities. One of the boys saw Leon's revolver. "Look dad, he's got a gun!"

The man stared at the weapon, Leon's 357 left to him by his father.

Samantha went forward and lit up the controls.

"That girl, she's not the pilot. Is she?" the father asked.

The Werewolf's Apprentice

"That would be me." Leon said.

"You're just a kid. They sent us a teenager with a gun stuck in his pants?"

"I'm twenty, age don't count for nothing out here. We're what you got. Those men out there are going to try to shoot us down. We came for you anyway."

"It's been a bad night," the mother said.

The sound of baying hounds echoed across the lake through the window.

Samantha yelled from the cockpit, "What's going on back there? Leon, get your ass up here."

Leon shrugged his shoulders and went forward to the controls.

Samantha stuck her smiling face into the cabin, "Good evening. I'll be your flight attendant. Snacks are in the cooler, no inflight movie, no wi-fi, no seat belts. In preparation for takeoff place the baby on the floor, brace her with your feet, hang onto the straps with both hands."

The Werewolf's Apprentice

"There they are." Leon said. "They lit up the boat."

Verbal commands to surrender floated across the water to the boat, it sped up, running for the opposite side of the lake.

"Get us out of here Leon."

Leon ignited the engines; oily blue smoke spread out over the water. The rough sound of eighteen cold cylinders shook the plane and echoed across the lake. The baby started crying.

The engines alerted the lights on shore. They turned to illuminate the black Grumman as it leapt out of the hidden cove. Frightened night birds filled the sky. Muzzle flashes lit up from the far shoreline. Bullets sang around the plane. Samantha lifted an AK-47 from behind the seat. She popped out the escape hatch and laid down wave after wave of tracers into the trees. Empty brass casings from the gun fell rattling down into the rear cabin. Her bullets set off small fires among the shooters. The baby wailed. The guns on the shore went silent.

"Cowards, that set them to running."

The plane lifted, Leon threaded a gap in the trees. He was wired up tight, mechanical, watching everything. A popping noise ran across the length of the plane as a lone gunman below found his target. A scream came from the back. "I'm hurt," yelled the mother.

Samantha dropped her gun and jumped into the cabin. The woman was leaning forward with blood running down her arm from a tear in the shoulder of her jacket. Samantha took her knife and cut the sleeve away.

"It's not arterial," she said, "we can fix it." She opened a first aid kit and applied a compress to the wound.

"Sam, I heard them talking to a plane on the scanner, we're gonna get company," Leon yelled, "Need you up here."

"Not now."

The Werewolf's Apprentice

Samantha looked at the man holding the baby, he was a wreck. One of the boys was crying in the back. The other was staring at his mother's blood-soaked jacket sleeve on the floor.

Samantha shook the boy hard. He was rigid. "YOU – get over here, hold this tight. NOW!"

The boy finally moved. Samantha spoke quietly as much for the mother as the boy. "Hold it, this way, right here. It's not bad, not bad at all. Mom's gonna be ok."

Samantha worked the compress over with tape.

The boy watched carefully.

Samantha looked into the woman's eyes for signs of shock. "We've stopped the bleeding. It missed the bone and your arteries, you're a lucky woman. You'll be ok. Don't move around a lot."

Leon's measured voice came from up front, "Sam, I need you."

The Werewolf's Apprentice

Samantha wiped the blood off her hands and crawled forward. She peeked out the escape hatch at the lights of an approaching aircraft. "I see him. Angels three, two miles off, closing fast. They see us, they're turning to follow. It's a turboprop, a fast one, twin engines."

Leon pushed the throttles full into the stops. "We can't outrun him."

Minutes passed in silence between them.

"Here he comes, he's on us," she said.

The aircraft buzzed over the top of the Goose at twice their speed, the old seaplane rocked in the turbulence. The plane banked around for another pass.

"He's gonna stick to our ass, call in his buddies and tag team us until we run out of gas."

The plane came around again. This time a pistol was hanging out a window aiming for the Grumman's engines. The gun started winking flashes of gunfire at the Goose.

"He's asking for it," Samantha said.

The Werewolf's Apprentice

Leon pushed the Grumman lower into the trees. "I'm killing the starboard engine, we'll blow smoke. Maybe he'll stop shooting."

Leon set the right engine mixture to full rich, fuel flooded the cylinders, the exhaust began blowing black smoke and flames. He feathered the prop and took the engine down to idle, the Goose started losing altitude. The chase plane pressed down on them like an unwelcome lover, closing on prey, waiting for the trees to do their work.

Samantha clipped a night scope on the AK, she rose out of the hatch into the smoke and wind. Her target floated like a giant toy in the milky green viewfinder, she saw the face of the pilot.

Her finger hesitated.

"Please don't make me do this."

Leon's voice came over the wind. "We're not going to make that next ridge, get them off us. NOW!"

The Werewolf's Apprentice

Everything became clear to her in the moment, serene anger flowed out from the dark place in her wolf-child core, it filled her with peace.

The wounded Grumman bared fangs as the AK danced in Samantha's hands. She released the full content of her weapon into the pursuers. The cockpit filled with falling brass, sound and smoke. The chase plane jerked up and away exposing her tender white belly. Samantha knew where to hurt them. She stitched holes all along the underside of the wings seeking out the weakness she knew was there. Misty streams of aviation fuel now trailed from the wing tanks. She ran a bead of tracers into the near prop. One blade parted away and spun off flipping end over end in slow motion into the night. Now unbalanced, the remaining blades shook the wing to pieces, the engine blew off its covers, it caught fire. The aircraft slowed, tilted over on its broken wing and entered a dreamy tumbling spiral towards the forest below.

The Werewolf's Apprentice

Samantha dropped down to her seat. The hot iron smell of the gun filled the plane.

Leon focused on the instruments. He tapped deep into the mechanical heart of the Grumman. He caressed the controls, stroking a machine built a lifetime before he was born, asking her for more. The Goose began to sing, she lifted, separating them from the approaching trees.

Leon relaxed in his seat, "You got him."

Samantha watched the falling plane slide into the trees tearing out a streak of hot metal and flame.

"Yeah, I got him."

"Now for home," Leon smiled as he said it, he banked the plane steep over the interstate. The plane took a sickening slide down towards the traffic below.

Leon turned his young eyes on the one beautiful thing in his life. How he loved her. Samantha was glowing. Her face the face of an avenging angel, windblown jet-black curls, confident strong hands, fingers tipped with long red nails wrapped around the barrel of her weapon.

He picked an open stretch between semis lined up out of Rochester. He dropped the plane in line, barely above the roadway and brought the Grumman down to seventy, matching the speed of the big rigs.

The father stuck her head in the cockpit.

"My God we're flying two feet off the road. Are we ok?"

"Cop radar, can't talk now." Leon skipped the plane over a pickup. The truck wobbled and slid off the road.

"Somebody just shit their pants," said Samantha.

Leon dodged a minivan. He turned to the ash white father. "They might send dope planes down from the Canadian border. Might be up there now. We ride down here, just off the pavement, slow. Radar can't paint us this low, we look like another truck with a hot motor if they are running thermal."

The Werewolf's Apprentice

"Will they find us?"

"The search area expands exponentially by our distance from the lake. Soon our numbers will overwhelm them. We find some lake in the boondocks, hide out a day or two."

"You do this kind of thing often?" the man asked Leon.

Samantha snapped a fresh clip in the AK and dropped it behind the seat.

"We do this sort of thing all the time," she said.

They landed on Spirit Lake and settled under a rusting dock house abandoned for the winter. Leon unpacked an alcohol stove and made coffee. The shivering children moved close, staring into the weak blue flames.

"Where are you from?" asked Samantha.

The woman spoke, "Reedsburg Colony, sixty miles north of Madison. There were fifty of us there."

"And?"

The Werewolf's Apprentice

"They found us, somehow. Two days ago, men in black trucks came. The highway was blocked with men with dogs and guns. For some reason they turned us around. Lucky, I guess. We were coming back from the frigging mall for God's sake. We saw the smoke and made it through the woods to the edge of town. They went from house to house, shooting and burning. They darted the young ones with tranquilizer guns, put them in black buses and hauled them away. We've been running ever since."

"Animal Control," said Leon.

The two boys watched as the story was told. "Where are we going?" One asked.

"A safe place," Samantha said.

The alcohol stove burned out. They sat in the dark watching the luminous hands of the planes' clock crawl through the night. Then the soft sound of a small aircraft over the woods, coming for the lake.

"Quiet, nobody move," said Leon.

The Werewolf's Apprentice

"I hear them," said the father. "It's them. They're going to find us."

"Nobody goes outside," Leon said. "If it's them, they're running thermal. Looking for heat signatures." Leon ran to the cockpit and turned on the instruments.

"Are we hot?" asked Samantha.

"No, the engines are at ambient." Leon pulled a silver blanket out of the locker, covered up and went out to the dock.

"They're coming back for another pass," he said. "They're running the other side of the lake."

The two boys picked up the fear, they looked worried. "Are they going to find us?" One asked Samantha.

"I won't lie. They may find us, but our odds are good, we're well hidden. There are hundreds of lakes out here, lots of them with boats and even float planes, they'll check those first. We'll be gone soon."

The Werewolf's Apprentice

The rising moon found Leon in the cockpit huddled over a map with Samantha. "We have to chance a day run, we leave at first light, their thermal will be poor during the day. I can get us way low, under their radar, that might be good enough."

Come the dawn, they took off to the west. Leon flew low and fast skimming the corn stalks, running down the valleys following rivers and hot steel railroad tracks, lower and faster than Parker or anyone ever dared fly a Goose.

The Werewolf's Apprentice

School's Out

They landed at Faith, a ground crew met them with a fork lift and wheeled the plane past a fleet of blue and yellow biplane crop dusters into the hangar. The logo on the duster's tail was a red heart on a circle with the words "Have Faith Kill Bugs" in white letters.

A man in an orange jumpsuit was fueling another Goose. Frank, the pilot, stood beside Samantha. Frank was young with a young man's beard. He wore a snug green flight suit with a grinning red fox embroidered on the shoulder. Hanging low in a holster was an Army issue Glock 9 automatic pistol.

Frank slid his fingers over the ragged holes in Samantha's plane.

"They almost had us this time," she said.

She felt Frank's hand on her shoulder. "Leon ok?"

"He's fine, we took one wounded, we got everyone out."

"That's good."

"I killed two men," she said, "I watched them burn. I didn't want to do it."

Frank stood looking at a shredded patch of aluminum near Samantha's wing tank. "They had it coming."

Frank's baby-faced co-pilot appeared in the window of the other Goose.

"All set Frank."

Frank brushed a piece of imaginary lint from his arm. He stared into the far sky, his eyes focused somewhere miles beyond the tree line.

"Ohio… I gotta get going."

A golf cart rolled into the hangar with Bone and a strange looking man with balding hair wearing a motorcycle jacket covered in zippers.

The Werewolf's Apprentice

"Get in, time for lunch." Bone said. They rolled out down the runway towards the woods. "Nice work guys, you've earned a little RnR. We're taking you off the planes for a while, something's come up."

"We heard about Reedsburg," Leon said.

"That's what this is about. I'm Chris," said the bald man, "everyone calls me Yoda."

"Yoda?"

"Yeah, that's me, Yoda. From operations, I am. Much you have done, much you have learned, young Leon. But more for you is there yet."

The cart took them to a log cabin near the edge of the field.

Inside was a table set with a mountain of ribs. Yoda sat between Parker and Bone.

"Forgive me, I have a tendency to ramble," he said. "Feel free to interrupt."

Yoda waved a white bone between their faces. "As you know, Animal Control has been reactivated. Reedsburg was the first. It's gonna start all over again. The bounty hunters are being called back. The Dog too. They're bringing in all the old gang. Jake's back in charge."

"If not the Goose, what?" Samantha asked.

"Your new job is to decapitate Animal Control. Gut the organization, both figuratively and physically," said Yoda. "The messier the better."

"That's your idea of RnR?" said Leon.

Yoda picked at the meat with his fork. He motioned to Bone.

"We have a list, names, aliases, locations," said Bone. "Your first target has been selected. It's an easy one."

"Targets?" asked Samantha. "I'm not an assassin."

"No, you are not." said Bone. "You are a soldier called to service. Their goal is nothing less than our extinction. This is a fight for survival. They're coming, it's only a matter of time before they find our sanctuaries, we'll lose everything."

Leon and Samantha felt the weight of his words.

Yoda softened, he placed his hands palms down on the table. "You two are the best we have. We need you to do this, for all of us."

"When?" asked Leon.

"As soon as we can get ready, two days, tops. We hit them now, while they think we're hiding in fear, weak and unorganized. Before they know our intentions."

"There must be some other way," said Samantha.

Yoda leaned forward, his eyes on them both. "These are not men, they are enemies. You know what they would have done to that family you brought in."

His words hung in the air between them.

Yellow eyes met yellow eyes across the table.

"The same thing they would have done to you."

"They keep the young ones alive, you know. For a while."

Yoda's words found their mark in her, the beast within awakened. She visibly shook as the orphaned monster rose. Samantha lost herself to the other, she crossed over, every part of her body began to sing. Yoda felt a terrible force rise in this young woman. Her eyes turned ozone blue and fixed on him. He felt the power of the Loup-garou, the carnivore were-beast of the dark forests of Europe. The killer of vampires, the ultimate terror.

"She has the gift," he whispered to Bone, "the one in ten thousand."

The transforming Samantha turned on the ancient power called charm. Parker, Bone and Yoda froze as paralyses gripped their limbs. Breathing became impossible. Their skin began to burn, they lost all control to the Alpha before them. She dominated her elders, they fell to submission, they shook and spoke in long forgotten wolfen tongues. A hundred years of lycan faces filled their vision. Leon stood outside of her gaze of control staring in awe as she grew and shifted. Her face took on the appearance of the wolf but still remained somehow very human, beautiful in a way, the silver stripes of the Garou-Alpha spread across her coat, long claws emerged, gleaming black, hard, sharp as atoms, with curved obsidian edges. She stood high above them all.

Samantha's voice came to them, deep and calm from a long lost place.

"Now it begins. I will find those who seek to destroy our kind. I will bring an end to them. They will fall before me knowing I am death, come to prey on their living flesh. Not one will escape me."

The Werewolf's Apprentice

The Dallas Hyatt

Dino Prince, top dog Texas Ranger with thirty werewolf pelts to his credit was half drunk at the Dallas Hyatt bar. A five-piece band in cowboy hats was putting out a fair rendition of Texas Swing. Dino was smiling and tapping his glass with the music. He felt the bump of a hip from the stool to his left.

He turned to see a younger woman pulling down the hem of a spaghetti strap black dress. His eyes fixed on her legs.

"Excuse me, is this seat taken?" Her accent, Atlantic coast, southern.

"Why no. Please join me, let me buy you a drink?"

"Thank you, my name is Sandi, with an 'i'," Samantha said

"I'm Dino."

The Werewolf's Apprentice

Dino saw a hint of tattoo riding just below the hem of her dress. Samantha lifted one strap ever so slightly. She wore her shining black hair cut just high enough to clear the top of her shoulders. The eyes were an inhuman radiant blue.

"Why thank you. Isn't that band great? I haven't danced in ages."

"Maybe we can remedy that." Dino said.

They put coasters over their drinks and went to the floor.

Leon slid down the bar and caged Dino's glass. He pricked a gel cap with a map pin and pinched out three drops of liquid rohypnol. He took another look at Dino's fat hands pawing Samantha and squeezed in three more.

Back from the floor, Samantha looked over Dino's shoulder at Leon checking the time. At ten minutes Leon got up. Samantha tossed back her drink and stroked Dino's leg with a single red nailed finger. He turned his empty glass over and motioned with his eyes to the elevators in the hall. Samantha tilted her head and gave him a woozy smile. She got up, leaving her purse at the bar. Dino slithered off to get it, he carried it back to her grinning like a crocodile.

Upstairs Dino fumbled with the card key. Samantha pushed him onto the bed and ducked into the bathroom. "I'll be right out."

Dino unbuttoned his shirt and leaned against the headboard. Samantha emerged in nothing but a black lace slip and sat on the edge of the bed. "How you feeling big guy?"

Dino tried to speak but his lips wouldn't move, he slurred out something about 'tits.'

Samantha sat up high lap dancing on Dino's crotch, she pulled her slip up over her head and tossed it to the floor. "Want some of this?"

The Werewolf's Apprentice

Dino's head twitched to one side, numb rubber lips formed into a twisted smile. He kept moving his tongue around in his mouth but nothing came out. Samantha raised his arm and let it drop.

She turned on.

Dino's eyes bulged in terror as the most beautiful woman he ever took to a hotel bed shifted into a shining tower of werewolf over his chest.

Samantha leaned into his unblinking eyes. She blew wolf breath in his face, she whispered in his ear, "I'm glad you're still awake, I wouldn't want you to miss a thing."

She stretched duct tape over his mouth and bared her fangs.

"Let's get kinky Dino."

The EMS boys stood at the foot of the bed in room three-eighty. Dino's severed head sat high on the pillows.

The Werewolf's Apprentice

His eyelids were stretched up to his forehead, pinned there with duct tape. Two Texas Rangers staying at the hotel stood over Dino's body parts. One of the rangers ran to the bathroom and puked up the undigested remains of an expensive lobster. He came back wiping his face with a washrag.

"What is this?" he said.

"This one's a real sickie, certifiable psycho," said the other. "Good luck forensics, they won't find nothing in this mess. Except for that baggie under his chin. That looks special."

Leon and Samantha drove in silence east on I-20 in a bone stock fifteen-year-old Chevy Cavalier.

"Sorry you pulled that one." Leon said, "I hated seeing him put his hands on you."

Samantha sat in her sweats fiddling with her hair. "I took a shower."

The Werewolf's Apprentice

She unlocked her cell and opened a list, she scratched out Dallas. "Never been to New Orleans," she said.

"Have to be careful now," said Leon, "after this they'll be alert. This next guy, Sonny, he's a family man, drinks an occasional beer with the boys after work, no mistresses. He's a true believer in the sanctity of marriage. A stern but loving father. His ass is mine."

"Any kids?" asked Samantha.

"Yeah. Two girls, twelve and fourteen."

"We let mommie and the kids live," she said. "We're not animals."

"Fine with me but we make them watch," said Leon, "I had to."

Samantha checked the GPS, "Yoda said ditch the car here in Monroe, take I-49 south. That'll take us into Slidell."

Samantha picked a used car lot hung with LSU pennants. The cars all had prices stuck on the windows in yellow tape. Leon got out with a bag full of money. Samantha rolled down the window of the Cavalier. "Get something good this time. No smokers, no green tree fresheners, they make my nose itch." She took off and turned out of sight.

Leon picked a silver 2009 supercharged Pontiac G6 with an aftermarket wing on the trunk. He paid in cash using a fake Louisiana license. He drove over behind the abandoned gas station where Samantha was wiping down the Cavalier.

"Another piece of crap, what's with that towel rack hanging off the back? That looks stupid."

"That's called a wing dearest."

"Useless thing it is, need to have, we do not." Samantha gargled her words.

"Like it, yes I do," said Leon.

The Werewolf's Apprentice

Slidell

Sonny Tubbs sat in the sun on his boat dock watching skiers jump wakes on Lake Pontchartrain. Bert Bennis came to the dock and took the chair beside him.

He tilted up the yellow jacketed book on the deck. "What you reading here?"

"Research, *Mongrels*, by this guy named Jones. Fiction, I think it's more fact than not."

Bert looked at the black wolf on the cover.

"You ever take a break?"

"It's all about perspective Bert, fresh ideas, new ways of looking at things."

"And what have you learned about our furry friends?"

"They drive old cars, American ones. They eat a lot of meat and ice cream. They're smart, way more than we give them credit for. Organized. Good at hiding, they prefer dumpy motels in poor sections of town and trailer parks. They move constantly."

"That's why I'm here Sonny."

"And?"

"Two days ago one of our guys who used to work Animal Control Dallas got chewed up in the Hyatt Regency. Maybe you know him from the old days, name is Dino."

"Yeah, I knew him. What happened?"

"They left his head sitting on a pillow."

"Nasty, any ideas who did it?"

"He was last seen headed for the elevators with a woman. Bar guy said she was smoking hot, never seen her before, high-end hooker type. It was a setup, guys like Dino don't get that lucky. One more thing, Dino's blood tested positive for roofie."

"You think she might be coming this way?"

"Nothing definite. Virginia is telling everyone to be careful."

"What does she look like?"

"Thin face, good looking, cheerleader body, early twenties, shoulder length black hair. Five-seven or so. That's it."

"Honey trap."

"Yup, she knew her man. The local guys called it psycho, I'm not buying. She had a job to do. She *ate* him Sonny, only the good parts. Left his guts behind in a pile on the bed."

"Woof-Woof time again. Guess I'd better dig out the silver bullets." Sonny laughed. "It's a one off, a lone wolf attack." He laughed harder, "Get it Bert? Lone wolf?"

"Don't be an idiot. She's not running around the woods in a fur suit. This was well planned, a calculated hit."

Sonny downed the rest of his beer, "We got the others, we'll get this one. They go stupid every full moon. They always screw up. Sure you won't stick around for a cold one?"

"No thanks I gotta run."

"Bert, did they leave anything behind? A note, something written on a mirror?"

"An ear in a zip-lock taped to his forehead. There was a dollar bill in there too. Had a lipstick stain, like the woman kissed it."

"Right or left?"

"I don't frigging know. What the hell does that have to do with anything?"

Sonny stared into the dark forest across the lake, he wasn't smiling anymore. "Years ago, we used bounty hunters. We paid five thousand an ear."

Sonny got quiet, staring at the trees, looking for unseen eyes, then, almost as if speaking to himself, "The old ones, they're back in business, this time they send their children for us."

The Werewolf's Apprentice

Sonny walked back to the house, werewolf book under his arm, to join the wife and kids for tuna sandwiches on the porch. Not too far away a couple rode by on a jet ski. He was a young man, maybe twenty, holding onto his waist was a pretty girl with a cheerleader body and short blonde hair.

The next day the jet ski appeared again, this time only the man was riding. He attempted a trick and fell into the water. While chasing the ski he surveyed Sonny's house and lawn. Sitting on the porch was an overweight plain clothes officer in a Hawaiian shirt showing a gun bulge. Next to the house was an unmarked navy-blue Crown Victoria, cop car. Sonny's wife came out and offered the man a lemonade. Leon crawled up on the ski and took off down the lake.

The Werewolf's Apprentice

Leon and Samantha lay on the bed in the Slidell Motel Six off the I-49 eating corn dogs watching "Friends".

"How do you feel about the lake?" asked Leon.

"It'll do, but we need more time. There's a resident motel closer to town. Let's move in there until we're done. Nobody stays at a Motel Six for more than a day or two. We might get red-flagged." Samantha went to the bath.

"Skid row it is. I'll get some Deet for the bed," Leon said.

Samantha talked through the door as she brushed her teeth. "You know Leon, I've been thinking, we may not have to do this one the hard way."

She came out of the bath straight off the cover of a Victoria Secret catalog, in red and black, tight, steaming hot. She crawled across the bed to Leon on her hands and knees. Her eyes flared yellow into his. She lowered down on him and slid up over his chest, lighting his skin with a thousand needle points.

The Werewolf's Apprentice

"I'm gonna get feral on you wolf boy."

Leon's anxious hands fumbled with her bra, "You wanna shift?"

"Nah, I want on top this time."

County Employee

Sonny was in his office reading up on Dallas. Only two videos offered any clues, one in the lobby, one from the parking structure. A stream of young women with the right body type came in the lobby about seven. Three of them might fit. A few were wearing tennis shorts, two of them had black hair in ponytails. The parking structure camera captured a busted Chevy Citation leaving sometime after the murder. Male driver, no passengers. An unusual car for a high-end hotel. Sonny emailed a deputy to check it against the Louisiana DMV for hits.

There was a soft knock at the door. A woman leaned her head in wearing a county health department badge. She was mousy looking thing, big oversized glasses, quite ordinary, no makeup, short frizzy blonde hair, in shapeless baggy green scrubs. She was carrying a white box with the Louisiana state seal on it and a clipboard.

"Detective Sonny Tubbs?"

"That would be me." Tubbs barely looked at her.

"Margo Gusti, County Health. That time again, I'm here for your annual flu shot."

"I thought we were getting those at the blood drive Thursday."

"No can do, that girl has the flu. That's a hoot. Not for her of course." She giggled. "I'm out trying to catch as many as I can today."

"I'm kind of busy right now."

"Don't be silly Mr. Tubbs. How busy will you be if you get the flu? What if you pass it around? You know policy for state employees. Every season, no exceptions. You just give me your arm and I'll be gone before you know it."

"Ok. Let's do it." Tubbs flopped his arm down back across the desk and worked the desktop with his free hand.

Margo swabbed his arm and gave him the shot. She put a little round flesh colored patch over the site.

"There you go. We're, all done. Not so bad, was it? Call this number if you experience any rash or tenderness at the injection site or burning sensations in that arm." She handed him a trifold sheet with an owl in a doctor's coat on the cover with a text bubble, "Don't Wait! Vaccinate!" Margo closed her case and shuffled out the door. Tubbs rubbed at the patch on his arm and went back to work.

Samantha dodged camera angles keeping her cell close and in front of her face. The police behind the desk were watching videos of car chases on YouTube. She left the station and got into a waiting Hyundai Elantra.

"How'd it go?" Leon asked.

"He was distracted, looking for us."

"My God you're something."

"You get the hair coloring?"

"Got it, and the extensions, I'm into red heads this week." Leon gave her a kiss. "This idea... You're frigging brilliant."

Samantha looked at her hair in the mirror. "A few more stunts like this and I won't have any scalp left, my hair looks like straw."

"The Tubbs family is going to have an interesting Friday night." Samantha wiggled out of the scrubs and stuffed them in a grocery bag.

Leon drummed the wheel with his fingers. "Maybe, Friday the Slidell cops go to TGI Friday's for happy hour."

The Werewolf's Apprentice

Samantha smiled like a guilty child. "Now that would be something to see."

"How about we go there and get some sizzling skewers or something? Catch the floor show."

Samantha stretched out her arms. "Why not, we're gonna silver up anyway, nobody's gonna notice a couple with red ears. Not after Sonny starts his doggie dance."

They drove to New Orleans. Leon and Samantha took a river view table at the Chop House and ordered the biggest au poivre steaks on the menu, medium rare.

Back in his office Sonny was working late checking his notes against the Dallas report on his screen. "This is all wrong," he said to himself. "It was the Hyatt, not the Hilton. It was last Tuesday, this says Thursday. Somebody's getting sloppy."

Happy Hour

Bert and Sonny sat at the TGIF bar drinking draft beers. Bert dug a soggy nacho out of the pile on his plate.

"Any more on Dallas?"

"Got a hit on the Cavalier, abandoned behind a gas station in Monroe."

"Any cameras?"

"We got nothing. Car was wiped clean, not even a candy wrapper."

Sonny picked a nacho off Bert's plate.

"Full moon tonight." Bert said.

"I've been reading up on that. Did you know only the newly infected and the true-blood werewolves lose control during the full moon?"

"I thought they were all the same." Bert grinned at the nachos.

"Nope, wolf children are special. Half human from birth. They shift at will, the moon works on them a bit, but they can control it."

"I can't believe we're talking about this." Bert said.

"People not believing is the ultimate cover. I gotta go to the bathroom, these nachos ain't sitting right." Sonny threaded his way through the crowd.

Leon and Samantha watched from their table near the door. They wore silver studs in their ears to suppress the moon shift. The studs began itching as the moon rose above the trees.

"Show time," said Leon.

"He's over fifty," Samantha said. "Dem virgin bones are gonna crack tonight. It's gonna hurt like hell, he's gonna go ape shit."

"Look at all those cops, we're biting the bear on the ass being here," said Leon, "we shouldn't have come."

The Werewolf's Apprentice

"We have to be sure," Samantha said. "Bone said no second takes. If he gets out of here alive, we have to finish him."

"Where did you put the keys?"

"Passenger side in a crumpled pack of Newports."

"Are you going to start smoking again?" asked Leon.

"Maybe."

A scream came out of the hall from the rest rooms. TGIF went silent.

The door flew open and Sonny staggered out, shreds of his shirt hanging from his arms, his pants were split open down around his knees. His legs were twisted, covered in thickening brown matted fur. His arms were bruised sausages, swollen from ruptured capillaries under his skin, his hands dripped blood where claws had pushed his nails out the tips of his fingers.

The worst was the head. His skin had split across the forehead revealing a portion of skull set in a partially formed wolf head. The rest of the face was a tangled mass of wolf and man. Human jaws set with twisted wolf teeth sticking out of bleeding gums.

Samantha gasped, "My God, he didn't make it all the way."

"No way I'm gonna eat that," said Leon.

Patrons started running for the door.

"Let's go," Leon said. "He's gonna run if the cops don't kill him." He and Samantha ran out past a screaming woman in LSU football jersey.

Sonny crashed through the restaurant knocking over tables and slashing out at people with his malformed arms. A big man in a Texas Ranger baseball cap tried to stop him. He fell to the floor with his cheek torn open to his chin.

"He's freaking, he's gonna run," Leon said.

Leon and Samantha hid among the trash bins behind TGIF, they took off their clothes, tossed them in a dumpster and shifted.

The Werewolf's Apprentice

They waited until Sonny tore his way out of the bar. He looked around the lot at terrified customers running for their cars. He took off. A group of cops watched him jump over a pickup and run into the woods.

Leon heard every word.

One of the younger men said, "Let's go get him."

An older officer held him back. "We don't want to play his game out there. Call SWAT and the dog truck, let the hounds find him for us. He can't get far."

Leon tracked Sonny crashing through the pine forest. They ran to the woods and moved towards his sound until they picked up the scent. He and Samantha split and ran parallel to Sonny's track. He was moving quickly but they soon closed. Sonny heard them on both sides making soft wolf noises. He ran faster.

They kept their distance, herding Sonny forward like border collies. He began to slow. They matched his pace driving him deeper into exhaustion and further into the forest.

They crossed a small field, Leon could see him clearly now. He was limping. Ahead rose a high ridge of cypress trees marking the border of a swamp. Sonny hesitated, he saw Samantha closing on his left. She was on all fours, her yellow eyes on him, low in the weeds moving in measured steps. Leon appeared to his right. Sonny spun, leapt, and disappeared. Leon and Samantha ran towards the swamp.

There before them were the steep walls of a concrete flood control channel. Sonny was on his knees in a running stream of water struggling to get to his feet. Leon slid down the side blocking his escape. Sonny started limping away to see Samantha coming from the other side. Sonny tried to climb the bank but slid back down. He lay in the cold green water looking into the faces of the young Alphas. Now he understood. These were a different kind, not the full moon crazies he hunted years back. He tried to stand. His rear foot was useless, swollen in the remains of a work boot. Wolf flesh oozed red and bleeding out between the leather shoelaces.

Leon slammed into Sonny's side with strength. Ribs broke, Sonny's lungs emptied. Samantha joined in, they worked on the ribcage until Sonny's nose and mouth foamed blood. Samantha pressed down on Sonny's neck with her hind foot pressing his face into the muddy concrete. Leon planted his claws on Sonny's head and tore off an ear with his fangs. Samantha ground down harder and harder until she felt the soft release of Sonny's neck vertebrae as they parted, finally the quiet snap of the spinal column, the windpipe collapsed. She stood on his neck until she was sure he was dead.

Leon and Samantha hid at the edge of the parking lot, stark naked and hungry from their shifts. The next lot over was a mob of cops and blinking red and blue lights. Dogs were baying on leashes. SWAT men were suiting up in body armor. The place smelled of idling diesels and cooked meat from the bar. The smell of the steaks burning drove Samantha and Leon mad with hunger. One by one customers were getting in their cars and driving off. Leon and Samantha crawled the maze of cars towards the Pontiac. Samantha lifted the door handle. No interior lights came on. Leon pulled them out in Monroe. She extracted the keys from the cigarette pack and started the car. They idled slowly out of the lot and joined the rest of the cars lined up going down to Slidell. Five miles later they pulled onto a frontage road and put on the sweats and flip flops they carry in the trunk. They hit the Wiener Schnitzel drive through for two Super Bowl family packs and a quart of chili.

Leon pulled the bun off his hot dog and soaked it in the chili.

"They'll be talking about this one for years," he said.

The Werewolf's Apprentice

"That flu idea was stupid, we can't afford stupid," Samantha said, "If those cops hadn't wasted all that time calling in SWAT we could have been in real trouble."

"You didn't know, it was supposed to happen at the dinner table in front of the wife and kids."

"We gotta be more careful," Samantha said, "We can't lay out patterns, patterns are dangerous."

They went back to their Deet soaked squat at the Duck Hunter Inn, Leon went to work wiping it down. Samantha brought in the bug out bag and handed Leon a manila envelope. He shook out a Metro-Cellular burner and a wallet, inside was five hundred dollars in dirty twenties, a passport, a prepaid ATM card and a Florida driver's license. "Arthur Miller, Homestead Florida. You can call me Art."

Samantha put down her chili dog and pulled the next set of instructions from Yoda off the dark web. "Let's get going Art," she said, "It's a long drive to Miami."

"One last thing," Leon handed Samantha one of the twenties and held out the bag with Sonny's ear.

"A kiss my love… for Sonny." She pasted on some lipstick and placed a perfect print on the bill.

Leon dropped the zip-lock into the afterhours book return at the Slidell library.

"That's two," Samantha said.

They stopped for rib eyes at an Outback Steak house full of overweight borderline diabetics. Come midnight they picked up the coast road and crossed into the Florida panhandle.

* * * * *

Bert was going through pictures from the TGIF scene. The pictures of Sonny were the worst he'd ever seen. He turned them over and stared out the window. A deputy came in and handed him an evidence bag. Inside was a zip-lock with a muddy ear and twenty-dollar bill sealed with a red kiss. Bert remembered Sonny's face and what he had said.

"Five thousand an ear, that's what we paid… …the old ones, they sent their children for us."

The Werewolf's Apprentice

In the Commonwealth

Truett Bridges walked in front of a map in a too cold office buried in a red brick colonial building in Falls Church, Virginia. In the room were three other men, Jake, Truett's boss, Lance and Noah.

"You guys ever hear of Bisbee, Arizona?"

Lance raised his hand, "Yeah that copper town, blew up twenty years or so ago, they were storing radioactive waste in an empty mine or something, it went Chernobyl."

"That's the story," Truett said.

"The story?" asked Noah.

"Everything you've ever heard about Bisbee until this day is a lie."

Lance raised his eyebrows, Nobel looked at his fingers.

"That incident was the accidental detonation of a dirty bomb built by werewolves."

Lance and Noah didn't move.

The Werewolf's Apprentice

Jake spun around in his chair looking at the ceiling. "Questions? Comments?"

Lance and Noah said nothing. Lance found his voice. "Please, don't stop now."

Noah pushed his thumbs together against the bridge of his nose and rolled back his head.

"There were three survivors, a Japanese woman, her father, how they made it out alive no one knows. A third man was arrested crossing the border at Douglas. He was glowing like a goddamn radium faced clock. Pegged the DHS radiation detector, they locked him up in an isolation unit in Phoenix."

"And the werewolves, how many did you catch?" Lance deadpanned the question to the room.

Jake pushed a notebook across the table. "He was the only one we found alive. Take a look at this."

Noah and Lance looked through pages of contorted six and seven-foot skeletons lying in the street. There were head shots of oddly shaped faces filled with teeth, others were tight shots of malformed paws with thumbs. Some were missing parts of their skulls.

Jake continued, "The guy in isolation 'shifted' as they say, killed two attendants and tore the arm off a nurse. Nothing could stop him, he broke out, the EMS guys ran him down with an ambulance."

Lance and Noah stared at the notebook with their mouths open.

Lance was the first to speak.

"What has this got to do with us?"

"We have a problem." Truett tossed two zip-lock bags on the table.

"What's with the ears?"

"We knew there were more out there. We formed a unit called Animal Control to hunt them down. Later we brought in free-lance, bounty hunters and off duty cops looking to make some extra money."

The Werewolf's Apprentice

We paid five thousand an ear. We killed hundreds of them. One month the body count went to zero, off like a switch."

"Where did they go?"

"No idea, not a trace for years, we got lucky a few times but nothing big, until this. A new generation. Hybrids, smarter, technical and well trained. The old ones were easy, wait for a full moon, go hunting. These are different."

Truett opened another folder. "Very different. We found the remains of a laboratory in a burned out basketball court at the Bisbee high school. There were fifty tanks in there, all smashed, inside the tanks were skeletons of partially grown humanoids. There was one there, a fully formed adult, she was the biggest lycan we've ever seen. She had the remains of a litter of werewolves inside her. Six to be exact."

The Werewolf's Apprentice

Lance looked through the pictures. "A nursery, a breeding farm."

"Yes," said Truett, "they may have found a way to genetically engineer the breed. Bigger, stronger and no doubt smarter than anything we've seen before."

"Did any get away?" asked Noah.

Jake was lost in reflection, he spoke, "We suspect there may be other Bisbees. Places where these young were moved to be raised and trained and to breed. We have to find them."

"And now we have this," Truett pushed two pictures across the table. One was Dino from Hyatt scene, the other was Sonny lying in the Slidell drainage ditch.

"Dino Prince, Texas Ranger, ran Animal Control for the southwest." Jake said.

Lance passed the Hyatt picture to Noah, "Messy."

Lance picked up the Sonny photo, he rubbed his free hand on his jeans. "What is that?"

The Werewolf's Apprentice

"Sonny Tubbs, Slidell Police, Animal Control, southeast, until last week he was clocking down his days to retirement. He was at a happy hour with his buddies, he went in the bathroom and came out looking like this, he took off into the woods, the dogs found him in that ditch. They kicked in his all his ribs and crushed his neck. We found mutant wolf prints at the scene, big ones."

Noah raised one of the bags, "The ears, the money. It's a message."

Truett was pacing now, "Damn right it's a message, from a goddamn werewolf death squad. God only knows how many are out there."

"What else you got?" Lance closed the notebook.

"One stinking clue and some lousy video. Sonny had a small round patch on his arm, the kind you get after a flu shot. A woman from county health made an unscheduled visit to the police station. As far as we know, she only saw one patient, Sonny. County said they didn't know a thing about her."

Jake spoke, "All we know for sure is there are at least two of them, a team. A man and a woman, early twenties, they stay in transient motels, drive crappy cars they ditch after every hit. You guys run on down there, talk to Bert. He was Sonny's partner. Pick up the trail and run down those fucks before any more of our guys get eaten."

"Any idea what their next target might be?" Noah asked.

Truett took over, "These are data virgins, digital ghosts, they don't exist in our system, or maybe they do, under a thousand planted identities. These are process killers, the end point of a supply chain delivering death door to door like Amazon Prime. The worst thing you can do is underestimate them."

The Werewolf's Apprentice

Lance and Noah stood to leave. Lance took off his reading glasses and spoke, "How many were in Animal Control? We need that list."

"At the peak, eight." Jake handed Lance a thick manila folder. "It's all here, video captures, pictures, names, addresses."

"What's with this pile of paper, don't you have this on a server?" Noah asked.

Truett looked at Jake. Jake nodded.

"I'm not telling you this, do you understand?" Truett said. "Ever hear of data entropy?"

The two men before him sat back down in rapture.

"The digital assets we have on these people can't be trusted. Every time someone accesses video, a jpeg or a document related to lycan activity the information degrades. We're not talking about documents disappearing, it's much worse, we're talking about tiny changes in the record that propagate over time. Nothing any one observer would notice."

Lance's eyes became animated.

"Two days ago, I wrote down the license plate off the car in the Hyatt video. If you look at it now the first two numbers are transposed, the video has degraded, just enough fog for you to think you got it wrong the first time. You believe the screen, correct your notes, update a file in a database, push out a corrected alert to every jurisdiction in the country. You become complicit in the deception."

"Genius," said Lance. "Digital dementia, the loss of institutional memory slowly over time. This is fantastic."

Jake examined his shredded finger nails, he looked worried. "These assholes are smart. They've started manipulating voice mails, text messages, social media posts. You could get a secure message from me ordering you to assassinate the mayor of Hartwell, Georgia. This is really bad shit, these werewolves, shifters, whatever the fuck you want to call them, have us going where they want us to go, seeing what we *want* to see. We confirm their deceptions as truth and see our truth as deception."

Lance and Noah got up again, Noah looked shaken, "We'd better get to Slidell."

The Werewolf's Apprentice

Saint George Hill

Leon and Samantha ditched the Pontiac at long term parking in Fort Lauderdale and took the shuttle bus to Miami International. Three hours later and one time zone east put them waiting for baggage in the steaming Saint Croix airport.

Samantha ran her fingers through the straps of her tank top. "Christ on the cross. It's hot down here. I'm panting like a dog."

"It's our underdeveloped sweat glands," Leon said. "We'll get some spray bottles in town."

"I'm gonna take off my shirt and lay my bare ninnies flat on that concrete." Samantha said.

"Can you tell me what Yoda said now?" Leon was panting now.

"At the hotel."

The Werewolf's Apprentice

The green and black minivan cab dropped them off at the Frederiksted Hotel. The open-air lobby was empty except for a clerk at the desk watching a calypso band on TV and two languid bodies slumped in wicker chairs playing dominoes.

"Yoda booked this dump?" Leon said, "If our room don't have air we're leaving, I don't care what the plan says."

"It has air." Samantha said. "Let's get settled and find that bar."

It was early evening when they took a beach front stroll, hand in hand along the sand up to the sounds and lights of the Lost Dog Pub and Pizza. There was a volleyball game on the beach, inside a few locals stewed to their eyeballs were talking loud at the bar. Leon ordered a triple pepperoni and sausage and joined Samantha at a cable spool table on the sand just outside.

Samantha looked irritated. "Seven thirty, he's late."

The Werewolf's Apprentice

"We are running on island time missy. Everyone's late down here."

A rasta man with foot-long dreadlocks and a Lion of Juda beard shuffled in from the street. He was wearing a gold lion head pendant hanging on a chain that could lift an anchor.

"That's our guy,' said Leon.

The rasta got a beer and scanned the room. He smiled at Samantha, walked over and took the extra seat.

"You look like tourists." he said. "Only ones in the room. Welcome to Fredriksted. Pizza is good here."

"Very meaty." Leon said.

"Zuma Dog, at your service. He picked a piece of greasy pepperoni off a slice. My taxi is outside. After the pizza we can take a little island tour if you like."

Zuma Dog's sun cracked Toyota rattled off away from town. The air conditioner was set to arctic.

The Werewolf's Apprentice

"What you doing down here Zuma Dog?" asked Samantha.

"Please, call me Zuma."

"A man named Randy Wallace arrived here five years ago from stateside. He liked the place. Fell in with the local voodoo people down out at Sprat Hole. They party hard every Saturday night up at this old planter's house. One night they gave him a drink, called the hammer. They brew it from tree bark they get up on the mountain. This Randy guy jumped up took off his clothes and danced around the fire for two solid hours and passed out. Later that night the voodoo guys blessed him, cut a scar tattoo into his shoulder. They said that he was a new man and must take a new name. Randy gave himself a name. That name was Zuma Dog."

"Are there any more of us down here?"

"I'm the only shifter on island, they got a few over on Saint Thomas. Puerto Rico is crazy with them. Cuban shifters came over there after Castro. They a savage bunch, they do not know peace."

"How is it?"

"It's safe, lot of voodoo people down here. Dead animal rituals and such. Blood and severed pig heads all over the place. If I get busy hardly anyone notices. Get this. Every full moon they go zombie on the hammer, run around the streets butt ass naked. I go wolfie on them and join the party, nobody cares. Every knee bows to the shifted Zuma Dog, they make offerings of meat to Zuma Dog. Crazed voodoo women give themselves to Zuma, they hump me like wildcats. I got it pretty easy here, the home office sends me money, all that Yoda wants me to do is keep tabs on 'that guy'."

"Where is the Moose?" asked Samantha.

"'The Moose. He stays low. He gotta place on Saint George hill. It's about two miles from here."

"House?"

The Werewolf's Apprentice

"It's a compound, old planter's house. Big stone wall, lots of dogs. Rottweilers. He's got three armed guards, one each shift. Always got one with him. I always wondered about the heavy security. I figured he was important. Yoda don't say shit to me about him so I figure he's a big fish. One look at you two and I sure don't wanna be the Moose. We'll be there soon."

"Let's not be obvious."

"No problem. We just drive by, I got all you need to know, house layout, guard times, what he do, his routine."

"The house is a problem, we can't get him in there," said Samantha, "When does he go out?"

"He goes to the store two, three times a week, but it's mostly the wife. He and the wife go over to Christiansted every Thursday night for dinner at Sparky's. No good, lots of people in 'Sted. We could try to get him in the car. But there's only one road, someone might see us. And we have the wife problem, I ain't gonna have nothing to do with hurting innocents. Jah would not approve."

"Is he ever alone?" said Samantha.

"Never, this is the best I got for you. Full moon he goes night diving off North Star beach. The water is so clear there the moon shines all the way down to the bottom. No tourists, no dogs. Just him and some muscle."

"That's the place." said Samantha.

"He a bad guy? What he do?" Zuma asked.

Leon leaned over from the back seat to Zuma. "Moose ran a death camp in Mississippi, they called it *The Pound*. Animal Control brought them any shifters they caught alive, mostly young ones, the children of murdered parents. They used them for genetic engineering, testing agents derived from Ebola and mad cow disease. They wanted a something that would run through shifters like smallpox and leave the humans untouched."

"Holy shit. What he doing down here?"

The Werewolf's Apprentice

"The shit got loose, wiped out this town in Mississippi named Scooba. Twenty dead bubbas. Their heads swole up like pumpkins, brains exploded out of eye sockets and ears. Animal Control came in, incinerated everything and bulldozed the roads in and out. They sent Moose down here until things cool down. Yoda says they're gonna start it up again. The Moose knows everything, we can't let that happen."

"Well you guys fix him up good." Zuma said.

"How many dogs?"

"Four or five. He's got a bunch of them."

"I'd like to infect them, let them do the job." Samantha said.

"Bad idea, that almost got us toasted back in Slidell."

Samantha twirled her hair with her finger. "Yeah, too complicated. The beach. We can eat him right there in the sand."

"Whoo ain't you guys some bad shit." Zuma Dog whistled.

"Yeah, we'll go full wolfie on his ass, it's isolated, and the woman won't be in the way." Samantha said. "How about the guard?"

"I'll take care of him for you." Zuma said, "But I ain't eating nobody."

"That pepperoni and easy voodoo hog meat made you soft Zuma," Leon said.

"I like it that way. I have my peace now, as much peace as our kind are allowed."

Samantha opened a pack of Newports.

"I guess I'll start smoking again," said Leon.

Samantha blew smoke out of her nose and mouth "I'm surprised you haven't already."

*****

The Werewolf's Apprentice

Two days later the full moon was at the horizon, rising to set the Caribbean Sea with sheets of diamonds. Zuma Dog led Samantha and Leon along a path of bone white sand. They emerged onto perfection. North Star beach lay as a quarter mile crescent of white coral bones before them. The beach found its end in an ancient lava flow of rough black rocks. Set back from the beach were a few scattered A-frame cabins, the remains of a failed beach resort. In front of the one nearest the beach was a ratty office chair buried up past the wheels in the sand.

"Here's the routine," Zuma said. "Moose will get here just after sunset. The guard always sits in that chair, he brings a cooler with beer and a radio. He's got a pistol, a Glock 9. Moose puts on his gear, one tank, no wetsuit. The guard smokes a little ganga sometimes. Moose has thirty minutes of air. He comes back, they get in the truck and leave. Same thing, every time."

"How long have you been tracking him? Leon asked.

The Werewolf's Apprentice

"Two years now, ever since I got the call to service. I'm glad you guys finally showed up. Tonight my obligation is paid in full."

"What's the plan?" asked Samantha.

"We hide in the cabin over there." Zuma reached in his backpack and pulled out three shiny metal tubes. "You go in there and shift. I got my silver ear studs, I'll take out the guard, you have your fun with the Moose."

"You gonna kill the guard? He's a civilian," said Leon.

"No, he's local, part time police, I hang with his sister. Everybody got a cousin or sister down here. I gotta live with myself after you gone."

They moved to the cabin. Zuma scattered their tracks. Leon and Samantha took off their clothes and shifted, waiting for the full moon to raise them to full strength. They lay panting in the night heat. Zuma Dog squatted next to them.

The Werewolf's Apprentice

The sound of two men's feet crunching on the coral path approached. One was in his late fifties, he had the body of a stronger man showing the first signs of age. He was carrying a dive bag. Next to him was a larger black man in a Cruzan police uniform, olive green sharp pressed shirt and gleaming white Bermuda shorts. Moose got into his equipment and waddled backwards in his fins into the sea. The guard sat in the chair, fished out a bottle of Schaeffer's and twisted off the cap.

Moose's mask and snorkel disappeared into the cove. Zuma raised one of the silver tubes to his mouth. He puffed his cheeks and blew silently into the tube. A tiny dart flew out and pinned itself in the neck of the guard. He reached back swatting a what he thought was a bug. He pulled out the dart and looked at the small patch of blood on his hand. Zuma quickly put two more into his back and upper shoulder.

The Werewolf's Apprentice

"He's ours now. Stay down, be quiet, let the medicine work."

The guard stood up holding his gun. He looked around. He walked towards the hut. Three steps from the window where they were hiding he stopped. The gun dropped into the sand. The man froze in place, he raised his arms to the sky and stood there trembling. His face took on a glassy sheen of sweat, his eyes rolled back to the whites, went wide and unblinking.

"What did you do to that poor devil?" Samantha said.

Zuma Dog smiled, "He be the zombie now. The darts tipped with spines of the puffer fish. Don't knock him over on your way out."

Samantha and Leon trotted out and took up positions on either side of the cove. They snuggled down in the white sand and waited. Time crawled by, the bubbles of Moose's breath appeared moving towards the shore. He stood up, pulled his fins off and walked through the shallows onto the beach. He stood there wrestling with the tank. From the edge of his vision he saw Leon rise from the sand.

Leon came at him at greyhound speed. Moose stood frozen, dropped his tank and began running up from the beach to the zombie guard. Zuma emerged from the cabin blocking his way. Moose frantically spun and ran for the path to the truck. It was there he met Samantha.

The two Lycans closed on him, backing the unfortunate Moose down back to the shoreline. The sand shifted away underneath his feet, he fell to his knees in the waves. Leon and Samantha descended on him, tearing at his arms and shoulders. Moose flailed at them like a bleeding rag doll. Blood flowed into the surf. Zuma Dog stood in awe, waiting for the death blow to the neck that never came.

Samantha and Leon withdrew, low and snarling as if to make their final attack. Moose dove back into the sea kicking wildly and stroking with torn arms as Samantha and Leon waded in behind him. Moose made it fifty feet out into the cove and treaded water in an ever-widening stain of his own blood.

Zuma stood beside Samantha and Leon. "Let him go, we have him," he said. "We bring the truth to him now."

Samantha stood high and called to the sea. Zuma snapped a leather bag from the string around his neck. The bag was tattooed with heathen symbols of the Voodoo priests.

"This is '*Tonton Macoute,*' strong magic, it calls those who will consume him."

Zuma waded out into the water towards the Moose, he poured blue and green crystals from the bag into his hand and cast them out towards the Moose. The crystals seethed in the ocean, spreading out a luminous slick towards the sea, surrounding the Moose. They washed over the Moose, a glowing stain spread over his chest into the bloody water.

Zuma retreated from the water.

"Now they come," he said.

The Werewolf's Apprentice

Barracuda.

Moose stood still staring at the beach. Behind him the surface to seaward formed into a cloud of foam and silver fins. Moose heard the sound, he saw them coming for him. He thrashed screaming towards the beach as the long silver fish tore into him at thirty miles per hour. Lean fast bodies with ragged razor teeth peeled muscle from bone. Moose began to go down. His last vision of this world was three forms on the beach observing his struggle.

Leon and Samantha went to the cabin and started dressing. "I guess that's the end of that," Leon said, "What we gonna do for an ear this time?"

"Do I have to think of everything?" she said.

Samantha pulled a hotel post card from her pack. On it was an island guy and mule with a straw hat on its head. On the back she wrote, *Having a wonderful time Jake, wish you were here.* She drew an ear with a cupid's arrow through it in red lipstick and stuffed the card along with a red kissed five-dollar bill in the zombie police officer's shirt pocket.

Leon and Samantha were eating at a beach bar the next afternoon. Moon Dog came in an sat down at the table.

"You guys gotta get out of here. Right now."

"What's going on?"

"My girlfriend, the sister of that cop? He told her a jet came in this morning, they parked it way off in a hangar. It was full of some federal guys from the states. They are everywhere. The airport is full of them. They won't let the cruise ship dock or nothing."

"It's them." Samantha said.

"You guys kicked over a wasp nest for sure. Every cop and taxi driver is looking for you, they got a five thousand dollar bounty on you guys heads. We gotta move fast."

"Is there somewhere we can hide?" asked Leon.

"No way, everyone knows everyone down here, five thousand is a lotta money, you won't last two days. I went

116

to the hotel, I got your shit in the car. You getting off this rock right now. There is this runner from St. Lucia loading up right now, he owes me. He's very good at avoiding authorities. Probably got a few hundred pounds of Colombian on board right now.

Samantha and Leon crossed the spongy gang plank onto a wooden inter-island transport at the Frederiksted pier. They watched as the crew swung a Mitsubishi minivan onto the deck and drop it down among the refrigerators and used cars. Zuma Dog followed them on board and counted out five hundred dollars to the captain.

"You the only passengers," he said. "These men will take you to Charlotte Amalie. No customs, no passports, nobody will know you are there, you can get a direct flight to the states. Saint Thomas is nice, you won't stand out, lots of tourists, two or three cruise ships a day, go to the Hotel 1829, they got steaks the size of catcher's mitts."

The Werewolf's Apprentice

Samantha kissed Zuma Dog. "You're a good man Zuma. Maybe we'll see you again if we come back for a honeymoon or something."

"Good luck to you., may peace and joy come to you both."

The boat's rattling diesel trailed a black smear of filth into the air as they left the tiny harbor. Samantha and Leon stood at the bow facing the thick salt breeze. Off in the distance the cloud ringed peak of St. Thomas' Crown Mountain rose above the horizon. A beat up Catalina 42 headed down island passed close, running fast under tight sails. It carried the name *Bad Girl*, at the wheel was a couple smiling and laughing. The woman waved, Samantha saw she was missing three of her fingers. *Wonder what happened to her?*

"What did you say?"

"Oh nothing, I was kind of dreaming that could be us one day," she said.

The Werewolf's Apprentice

Leon pressed Samantha against the prow, he put his arms around her waist. Her black hair flowed in the wind around them, her animal scent called to him.

Leon brushed a curl of hair from her face, "I'm no De Caprio and this sure ain't the Titanic but no man ever felt more love for a woman than I do now."

The Werewolf's Apprentice

Fire and Fury

News of the Saint Croix incident went through Animal Control in Virginia like a firestorm. Jake had now chewed his nails down to the bleeding quick. Truett paced the floor dialing and redialing Lance's cell phone.

Jake was impatient. "Where is Lance? I'm worried, maybe they got him too."

Truett hung up the phone. "He'll see the caller id."

Jake ranted at the map on the wall. "Moose was under deep cover. He had rottweilers and armed guards. They got him anyway."

Jake waved the postcard in his hand.

"And now this, '*having a great time* Jake*, wishing you were here.'* These animals know my name. The bastards... These sons of bitches... They won't stop until *our* ears are in a jar. Dallas, Slidell, Frederiksted, no pattern, vast

120

distances. Nothing but a trail of abandoned cars and dead bodies."

Truett scanned the report, "We've locked down that island tight. We're checking everything that breathes going in and out of Saint Croix. Nothing. They have to be on the island," he said. "We even locked down the pet carriers."

Jake stared at the island on the map. "They're long gone. Those miserable rocks are US territory they may as well be in Miami."

"We did get a hit on the cars. Both of them. We're interviewing the used car lot guys now." said Truett.

"Let me guess, the office cameras had a mysterious failure shortly after the transaction."

Truett sat down and rubbed his eyes. "These guys are like nothing we've ever seen. They move fast but don't appear to be in a hurry. They are imaginative and ruthlessly savage. They vary their methods, they get everything right every time, they're invisible. I'm scared Jake, really scared.

The Werewolf's Apprentice

For the first time working here I don't feel like the company can protect me. That Moose cover was the best we can do and they took him with such ease."

Jake drummed his fingers on his desk, he pushed desk toys and papers around in front of him. "I refuse to live the life of a hunted thing. We keep up the chase, go prophylactic. Full security for the other top five. No rent-a-cops like on the island. These guys are smart and careful, but they won't stop, we'll limit their targets. Make them come to us. They'll make a mistake. Get Lance on the goddamn phone, tell him and that Noah guy to get their asses out to LA."

"I have an idea."

Samantha opened the cane slat blinds in their room at the Hotel 1829. Charlotte Amalie was waking up to another balmy Caribbean morning. Across the harbor the taxis were lining up for the Cruise ships. She was wearing satin midnight blue Chantilly lace slip. The salt breeze blew back her hair and eased the fabric against the contours of her body.

"Can we come back here later? When this is all over?" she said.

"I promise," said Leon, "How many more days are we gonna stay here? Yoda keeps telling us to stay put and relax. Get that burner. It's buzzing again."

Samantha opened the text message. "New net id."

"Must be urgent," Leon unpacked the laptop."

He opened the browser onto the dark web and keyed in the new access code. "Change of plans."

"What?"

Leon read the message, "It's Bone. Animal Control has activated a kill team. Targets are being hardened. All action cancelled until further notice. New target, details to follow on your arrival Los Angeles. Use three cars. Change @ Atlanta, Houston, Phoenix, take bus to LA. Replace burner

SIM with SIM card #12. Go dark until further notice. More instructions to follow by email."

Samantha lit a Newport and blew the smoke out the window. "We just hit their inner circle. They got the love note," she said. "I bet it scared the shit out of them."

"They'll be ready for us next time," said Leon, "We need to be careful."

"Let them come." said Samantha. She cracked open the burner, replaced the sim card and flushed the old one down the toilet.

An email buzzed in on the laptop. "It's Yoda We're leaving, today," she said.

The couple rotated out of their Florida Ids and became Allen Adam and Misty Tanner residents of North Hollywood, California.

Samantha flopped down on the bed, "Misty Tanner? What kind of porn trash name is this?"

The Werewolf's Apprentice

Leon pulled her slip up and took tiny wolf nips all around her navel with his teeth, "Come to Adam, my trembling nympho goddess, I wanna tend to your crop circle."

Samantha swatted him away, "Maybe later tiger boy. We got a cab on its way, get dressed. We're expected down at the docks."

The cab dropped them off at the cruise ship terminal, they sat in the local Hooter's franchise next to the wholesale liquor stores. Samantha hung her wolf's head pendant outside her shirt. They waited.

An older couple walked by their table, they were quite ordinary in every way. The man handed Leon a bag. In the bag were three tourist shirts, two Carnival Cruise reboarding passes assigned to Misty Tanner and Allen Adam and a car claim ticket from a Port Everglades lot.

The Werewolf's Apprentice

City of the Angels

Arriving in LA by bus is either the beginning of the end or the end of a beginning. The City of the Angels greets all comers with a kiss or fang, awarded to each new arrival according to their ability to pay. Currencies accepted range from money to beauty, with youth and innocence always in demand.

Samantha was sleeping mouth open, head against the window. Leon was fixated on his phone map waiting for the fifteen miles of red in front of them to go green. Samantha woke.

"Are we there yet?"

"No."

"When's the next rest stop?"

"No more rest stops, next event is the release of les misérables at the Fontana Outlet Mall."

"I can't stand it. Yoda said go to LA, this is close enough. Let's get out here and buy a frigging car. Nobody walks in LA," said Samantha.

"Only a nobody walks in LA," said Leon.

Samantha poked Leon in the arm. "And no towel rack this time. Those things look stupid."

"They're called wings and have legitimate aerodynamic qualities."

"No towel rack." Samantha crossed her arms and looked out the window.

"Ok, Ok, Don't crawl up my ass."

Samantha licked her finger and held it to her nose. "I gotta brush my teeth, my mouth feels like an algae farm."

The bus stopped in a cold as shit parking lot swept with winds of smog and sand down out of the high desert. Off to the west the eternal false dawn of the city reflected off a Pacific marine layer. Leon and Samantha took their place in the aisle along with the busted out retirees returning from a free food and hotel junket at Whiskey Pete's Hotel and Casino.

They left the shuffling crowd in the parking lot over to Chili's and ordered four racks of baby back ribs and a chaser of cheese stuffed fried jalapenos.

"What now?" Samantha asked.

"Use our last bottle of Deet on a cheap motel bed, get up, buy a car, drive to the beach and wait for Yoda."

"I need some clothes," she said.

Leon woke early. He opened the window onto the trash filled swimming pool of the Ontario Cactus King Motel. The inland empire sun poured through the glass in a wave of nuclear heat and light. It felt familiar to him. Samantha was bed snoring with her head sandwiched between two pillows.

"I'm going car shopping," Leon said.

"Uhh, ok. No wings."

The Werewolf's Apprentice

Leon went to the office and called a cab on the desk phone. Werewolves only use cash for cabs, no Lyft or Uber. This driver knew every used car lot in Ontario. Leon had him go to the biggest independent. He picked out a gigantic high mileage red Ford Expedition with running boards that snapped out from under the truck when he opened the door. It was an out of state auction job with paper tags good for ninety days, a key factor in car selection for burner cars.

Samantha was at the office ready with their bags when he arrived. He kissed her and popped the rear gate with the remote.

"God whatta monster," she said.

Leon smudged the numbers on the paper plates with a marker.

"Good air, power everything," Leon took the wheel.

He felt his past creeping up on him as they crested the rim of the basin and began the long drop into the heart of the throbbing pink monster that is LA. In the distance the nest of strawberry and gold towers of downtown stood like alien space ships feeding off freeway tentacles laid out to consume the earth.

In his head Leon heard his mother and father talking in their living room in Santa Monica. Scraps of low conversation. Names, *Andrea, Jessie, Sylvia,* places, *Pan Pipes, Rose Avenue, Trinity, Bisbee,* words he was never meant to hear. Forbidden words. Need to know words. Words kept from him to keep him safe.

"Only one hour with them, that's all I want." said Leon.

"With who?" Samantha asked.

"My parents, I grew up here."

Samantha sighed, "We don't get a past. We could go back to Faith tomorrow and find nothing to say we were ever there."

"This is never going to end," said Leon. "I feel so old."

The Werewolf's Apprentice

"Orphans grow up hard," said Samantha, "That's why they put us together, that's why they sent us."

"What do you think is next?" asked Leon.

"Don't know, something off the plan, a shock target, unexpected and possibly well known, even famous. Something that will get some press. Increase the problem space for those guys in Virginia. Maybe scare them into making a mistake. They're human, one or two might panic and give us some easy hits."

They checked into a faded avocado flavored motel near the 405 freeway on Washington Boulevard. Next door was a recycling shop surrounded by a bathtub rig of scavengers and their shopping carts. The room smelled of Lysol, stale beer and cigarettes.

"You ever feel like you've looked through the same window sometime, somewhere before?" he asked Samantha.

The Werewolf's Apprentice

"It's a wolfie thing," she said.

Leon paced around the room, "I'm crawling out of my skin not knowing. Check in with Yoda, see if he has something for us."

Samantha brought up Tor on the laptop.

"Wee-hoo," she said, "This girl is positively clairvoyant. I was right, you'll never guess."

"Who is it?"

"Dog the Bail Bond Hunter. Star of that TV show. He ran the bounty hunters for Animal Control. He was field guy too, fifty-pelts. He's shooting out here for a month."

"Fifty pelts? He's been a very bad boy," said Leon, "I'm gonna snap his arm off and beat him to death with it."

"Don't get creative, they're on to us now, we take him fast and clean, a few bites of the good parts, all the cops get is an ear, a five-dollar bill and a mess to clean up."

"This guy is special."

The Werewolf's Apprentice

"Very special, too special perhaps, I know they are waiting for us," Samantha yawned. "These guys aren't stupid. A juicy high profile target like the Dog might be bait."

Leon looked out the window at two bums fighting over a trash bag full of cans. "When do we start?"

"Yoda says settle in, relax, we move to a safe house in Van Nuys tomorrow. Looks like we have jobs in the movie business."

Show Biz

Next afternoon found Leon and Samantha in the valley at Mom's Bar-B-Q on Vanowen shredding four fried chicken platters and a side of ribs. The cooks looked nervous.

"This is some serious bird," said Leon, "Right down the street too."

Samantha scraped a platter of bones into the trash. "Just in from Bone, three this afternoon, BugHouse productions. Charlie Boxer is the guy. Bughouse does paranormal shows, *Terror of the Teen Wolf, House of Bones, Sinister Outcomes,* and a certain bounty hunter show."

Leon threaded the Excursion through a maze of porno stores, strip clubs and edible underwear shops along Oxnard boulevard. At the end of an undistinguished street lined with dumpsters and homeless tents they found a small lot filled with trucks and mobile video vans, each one marked with a giant black bug eating a school bus. "Must be the place," Samantha said.

Charlie Boxer sat behind a huge maple desk surrounded by glossy photos of paranormals. A full up werewolf suit hung on a rack in the corner. Leon was staring at it.

"*Teen Wolf Too,* that's one of ours. You see it?"

Samantha turned up her nose, "We don't approve of shifter exploitation movies."

"It's all in good fun. LA is a great town. You won't believe the shit we get away with around here. You can stand out front of the Chinese Theater under a full moon fully shifted, fangs and all and people tip you five bucks for a selfie. Then there's Halloween, *everyone* comes out to play."

"We're good with animals, want to work the Dog show," said Leon.

The Werewolf's Apprentice

"That Yoda, he's funny. He set you up with that line?" Charlie unloaded a Kool One Hundred and lit it up, "Here's the deal."

"We carry a few open union cards for guys that ain't in the union. They look legitimate, work history, pay stubs, social, addresses, everything. I loan these cards to whoever's working that week. Untraceable, not legal, nobody cares." Charlie passed over two plastic credential pouches.

"Lois Legato, Bruce Willard, welcome to the crew. Take these to Carl over in special effects he'll razor in new pictures."

"We don't like pictures," Leon said.

"Carl knows all about that, they'll be of rather poor quality, sloppy work, over exposed. Gel cap behind them, crush it before you dump them. Pictures go away. Pay attention if someone looks too close, union reps are the only ones that might do that. Security cops just eat and

136

stand around a lot, don't worry about them. If one of them does pay extra attention to you, make sure tell me. We'll take care of it."

"Carl's out there in the shop somewhere. He'll show you what you need to know. Monkey work, cables, dragging coolers with drinks and stuff. Nothing technical. As grunts it is expected for you not to know much of anything. Be humble, look dim, you'll fit right in. Any questions?"

"When do we start?"

"Dog's not in town right now. He's coming in for a shoot Monday in Boyle Heights. Since you're free, I wish you would help me out. I'm short extras for tomorrow night. Pays $450 a head. It's a music video shoot down at the Venice beach skate park. Loads of fun."

"We'll do it," Leon said, "I've always wanted to be in the movies."

The Werewolf's Apprentice

"Great, you guys relax, we'll send a limo around at four tomorrow afternoon. Loose clothing, shorts, casual beach attire. Usual stuff, the band plays, the crowd dances and waves their arms. It's catered of course."

Rose Avenue

The limo rolled into Venice down Rose Avenue past bright clubs and restaurants towards the skate park.

"I grew up here." said Leon. "My dad had an office up here on the left."

"What did he do?"

"He was a paranormal video guy. People would pay him to contact the sprits of dead relatives. Ghost hunting was big back then. Things got hot, we almost got caught. They had some money, we moved to Knoxville and hid out in the suburbs."

"What happened?"

"Animal Control came one night, I was the only one that got away. Bone rescued me. Took me to Faith. Not much of a story, huh?"

The Werewolf's Apprentice

"I grew up in Mount Pleasant, across the Cooper river from Charleston," she said. "Mom and dad had a charter fishing business. They took some clients out, just like any other day. That morning a stranger came to the door, he said his name was 'Christopher.' Mom made me repeat that name every day of my life. It meant there was danger and I should go with him. I never saw them or home again." Samantha became quiet, she turned to the window chewing the tip of her thumb.

"Those men took everything from me."

Leon watched her breathing rise and fall in patches of vapor on the glass. She was far away now, years past, standing at the Shem Creek docks waiting for her father to come in. Where shrimp boats hung with batwing nets tug at their moorings and the air smells of creosote and salt marshes.

The Werewolf's Apprentice

The limo dropped them off at Windward Circle a short walk from the skate park, Carl was in the costume truck.

"Hey guys, right on time. Jump in here and we'll get you all set up. Everyone else is over at the park, the band's warming up."

The van smelled like latex balloons. Carl took Samantha's height and unzipped a garment bag. He held out a hairy wolf costume and a rubber head with a mouth filled with giant yellow fangs. "This should do just fine."

Samantha struggled with zipper, "You're shitting me. Is this Charlie's idea of a joke?"

Carl held up a large toothed comb, "Hold still, I gotta brush out your fur, you wanna look good for the cameras."

He stood back, "There, much better."

"Oh, almost forgot the booties and gloves," Carl slipped a pair of hairy rubber wolf feet over their shoes and handed them each a pair of black rubber claw gloves.

The Werewolf's Apprentice

"Look at you. Never better." Leon said. "Let's go dance."

"What's the band's name?" asked Samantha.

"Los Lobos," Carl said.

"Of course. Something about wolves being hungry?"

"That was Duran-Duran," Leon said. "Hungry Like the Wolf."

"Shut up Leon."

"Careful on those steps, you kids get down there and have a good time."

Leon patted Samantha under her tail as they walked to the stage. "You looking good tonight mama."

Samantha smacked him in the head with her rubber claws, "This is so redundant. I'm sweating to death in this thing."

"This gives me an idea," said Leon. "Let's hold on to these for a while."

Boyle Heights

Lance and Noah parked their LAPD motor pool Crown Vic just down the street from the mobile video unit. Across the street was *Leo's Carnitas* taco truck. Leo sliced his mighty blade along a spit of rotating pork catching the meat with the tortilla in his hand. The final flourish, a nipping swing at the pineapple at the top of the rack into the air and the catching the yellow slice in mid-air.

"There's the boss, let's go check in." said Noah.

Carl looked them over. "Where's Eddie? He was booked for today."

"Eddie got a summons. Last minute," said Lance.

Carl looked at the clipboard. "Talent is due here in a few minutes. No action scenes today it's all background."

"Who's the guy?" Noah asked.

"Some chump named Clarence Bagwell, grand theft auto, pervert rapist, dope peddler."

The Werewolf's Apprentice

"Where is he?" asked Lance.

"If we told you that, wouldn't have a show now, would we? Here, initial this time card, I want you to run off those tourists up there in the yard."

Samantha walked by Carl with a battery pack for the cameraman. He motioned her over.

Carl didn't look up from this clipboard. "Nice shade of blue with the hair, that ID pix is out of date already."

He nodded up to Lance and Noah pushing the Dog fans off the yard. "Don't look, new guys. Never seen them before."

Carl waved his hand to the remote truck, Samantha shook her head.

"No problem," said Carl, "I'll tell Leon, stay with the camera guy, look busy."

Dog and the bail bondsman arrived in a limo. They got out and spent an hour walking around the house checking the mail drop, looking through windows and knocking on doors. Some lady made an entrance in a Ford Explorer and yelled at them in Spanish. They did two more takes of her yelling and taking pictures of Dog with her cell phone and pushing the bondsman around. Carl called it a wrap.

On the way back to the shop Carl called Charlie on the cell, he turned his attention to Leon. "We use maybe fifteen rent-a-cops on these remotes. All the same bunch, fifty-five plus easing out towards retirement. Those two don't fit. Too young, only old guys do the shoots. I saw them talking to Dog. My guys know better, if they did that Dog would have me get rid of him. Smells funny."

"Who are they?"

"Undercover, probably looking for you. Go home. Oh, Charlie says you guys just got fired."

Samantha was paddling around in the shallow end of the pool at the safe house on Victory. Leon sat on the edge with his feet in the water swishing around with his feet.

"What do we do?" Asked Samantha.

"Don't know. I'm feeling very alert. It's that wolfie survival thing. Non-specific wolfie alertness. I don't like that feeling. This plan sucks. We need the Dog alone."

"We have time," said Samantha, "I kind of like this place. Maybe I'll do something with this hair."

"Dog has a place in Hawaii, we could wait him out and follow him there," she said.

"Another island, like Saint Croix. Coincidental air travel following the target. Yoda won't like it."

"I've been thinking," said Samantha, "Those two guys, seems kind of lucky for them to show up exactly the first day we are on the job. Yoda cools the plan and sends us over here. These guys show up. Don't seem right, too convenient. Too many moving parts for me, and we seem to be at the center."

The night timer killed the pool lights. Leon slid into the water. Samantha floated in on him and locked her hips around his waist, put her arms around his neck and pulled herself tight against him.

"Dog can wait."

"Fifty pelts, fifty, I want that mother." Leon said.

Samantha undid her top.

"Dog can wait."

Leon tried to speak but Samantha was on him now.

She peeled apart the Velcro on his cutoffs.

"Handy stuff this Velcro," she said, she pushed his shorts down his legs with her foot.

She began shifting, slowly. Gradually becoming a perfect object of desire moving to the shallow end of the pool. Leon followed in a trance. He felt cocaine animal surges all through him, every nerve was singing. She rose dripping wet out of the water and profiled. Leon lost his mind.

The Werewolf's Apprentice

They lay like spoons in the big bed. Leon listened to the soft sounds of her breathing.

Outside the popping blades of an LAPD helicopter circled a block away lighting up the world with a Nightsun search light.

"Another screwed loser, running, hiding, breathing hard, hiding somewhere in the dark."

The burner phone ringtone went off filling the room with the first two bars of Duran Duran's "Hungry Like the Wolf" over and over again. Samantha slapped the bed with her arms.

"That noise is getting real old Leon."

"I got it," he said.

"What is it?"

"Text from Charlie Boxer, an address in Sherman Oaks. There's a van. He says get there around noon and call him."

"And?"

"No details, he only says its orders from Yoda."

The Werewolf's Apprentice

"Must be new business," said Samantha.

*****

Early evening the next day Lance and Noah were returning from a Dog shoot high in Topanga Canyon. Lance was irritated. They'd been tailgating a slow as shit rust holed Ford Windstar for two miles. As they approached a blind turn the minivan slowed even more, pulled slightly to the right giving up a half lane, a hand reached out and waved them around. Lance ignored the double yellow and floored the Crown Vic. A huge Dodge Power Wagon with tandem wheels blocked him on the curve. Lance swerved into the guard rail. The Dodge turned dead center into the side of Lance's car. The Dodge crumpled up the Crown Vic door with its pusher bars.

The Werewolf's Apprentice

Leon looked down from the Dodge into the terrified eyes of Noah kicking at the jammed passenger window. Leon pressed down hard, the Crown Vic groaned as it rose against the rail. The windshield shattered into a thousand bits of glass, Noah grabbed the windshield wipers and tried to pull himself out. The rail posts gave way, the Crown Vic eased in slow motion over the edge and down into the three-hundred-foot canyon with Noah screaming and flopping around on the hood. The old cop car turned end over end, the gas tank ripped open on the rocks below and caught fire.

Leon left the Dodge idling in place, Samantha picked him up and drove back towards the Valley. The fire below was advancing as they passed.

"I saw his face, he looked right at me," Leon said. "That guy didn't wanna die."

"Yeah? Neither do I," she said. "He was a bug."

"What makes you and me any different from those two guys?"

Samantha fumbled for a Newport. "Fangs."

Animal Control

It was a warm afternoon at Animal Control in Virginia, Jake was at his computer eating a BBQ brisket and spicy curly fries. Truett entered the office and shut the door.

"Lance and Noah had an accident," said Truett.

Jake stared at the screen, "What kind of accident?"

"Car accident, they went off the road, fell into a canyon. The car caught fire."

"That's lovely," said Jake. "We get any ears in the mail?"

"Not funny."

"I guess it was a long climb down to the car."

"It's them," Truett said.

"Goddamn right it's them," said Jake, "They had three outstanding targets. Odds were on the Dog. We knew they were heading west."

"But they didn't get the Dog. They got the guys we sent to protect him. They're always playing offence. They knew."

"Does Dog know they were our guys?"

"Nope, they were undercover as security cops."

Jake walked to the white board, "What next? What next?" He paced pulling and snapping the cap on a sharpie.

"Ok, let's review." He pointed to a map spotted with post-it notes.

"First hit, Dino Prince, Dallas Hyatt. Drugged, sloppy drunk and horny, that was practice."

"Number two, Sonny Tubbs, our little friends get creative. Nurse injects tainted blood before the full moon. Ends up half werewolf in a ditch with his ribs kicked in. Poor Sonny, I liked that guy. Family man too."

"Number three. The Moose. Eaten alive by a swarm of barracuda. He had a 7/24 security detail and a pack of rottweilers, they still got him."

153

"The last of the list…" Jake opened a folder and pasted three more faces on the board.

"The Dog, California, Henry Powell, Vermont, and Mike Harmon. Where is Harmon? We don't have anything on him."

"Powell's dead, his wife shot him two years ago. Harmon's last known to be in southern Georgia around Savannah, maybe Charleston, he went off the grid five years ago. No idea where he is."

Jake tapped the map with the sharpie, "Maybe *Harmon* was the first."

"Don't fit the ear story, might have been a lone wolf attack."

"That's funny Truett. Let's assume he's dead or in Bangkok or somewhere."

"What about the Dog?"

"Don't tell him shit, he's still our bait. I want his ass totally covered. I want to know if he gets bitten by an insect. They still want him, they'll be back, I'm sure of it."

"The real issue here, if I may be so bold," said Truett, "is that you and I are probably the last on their list."

Jake slammed the cap of the sharpie against his palm, "We'll see about that."

"Jake, I'm taking a few days off, I'll be back in Monday. I'll tell Arthur to set up the Dog detail."

"No problem, where you going?"

"Up to the mountains, get away from this for a day or so, hang out. I'll be on cell if you need me."

Truett went back to his office, put the family pictures into his messenger bag, left his cell phone and a note to Jake in his desk drawer along with his card key.

The Werewolf's Apprentice

Mount Pleasant

Connecting Charleston proper from the north barrier islands is a bridge. Ramping up on the Meeting Street ramp was a wretched Kia Sorrento wagon. The rear of the car was jammed to the windows with bags of aluminum cans, dirty clothes and two filthy sleeping bags. The floor behind the seat was covered in fast food bags, crushed cigarette packs and fried chicken boxes filled with bones.

"Deep cover, Yoda said, look like homeless people he said, smell bad, this is a deep as I wanna get." Samantha rolled down the window and flicked a Newport off into the Cooper River below. "Feel that humidity. We better leave the windows down tonight. This car is gonna stink tomorrow."

"We have an upgrade waiting in Wando," Leon said.

Samantha looked out over the swampy estuaries that fed into the sea, "I feel creepy coming back here. My chest is getting tight. Let's get this done fast, I never want to see Shem Creek again."

They dumped the Kia in Wando at a rundown gas station with watermelons on the porch. A gentle old man dressed like he sold chickens for a living moved the Kia out of sight into a hundred-year-old pigeon roost of a garage. He handed them the keys to a Mercedes 500 parked in a discount store parking lot across the road. Leon and Samantha loaded up on fresh clothes at resort mall off the Savannah highway on the way back to town.

Samantha sat on the edge of the bed at the Sullivan's Island Best Western and called a number. Leon listened in on the speaker phone.

"Captain's Courageous Deep Sea Charters?"

"We'd like to book the boat, exclusively for one day."

"Yes, we can come in this afternoon."

Samantha and Leon entered a small blue office in a strip mall near the docks on Shem Creek. A neat looking sixty-something lady with reading glasses tethered to her neck on a gold chain was on the phone.

"I'm Amada Collins, Mike's wife, just a moment," she said. "Be right with you."

Leon walked around the small room looking at the trophy pictures. He found the captain's license. He took a snap of it with his cell phone. Next to it was another of Captain Mike with a group of men posing around a dead boar. One face stood out among them all, a man kneeling with his arms around two dogs. A face that Leon would never forget.

"Decker."

"There, that's all done. Are you the ones that called for a charter?"

"Yes, thank you," said Samantha, "we want a private trip."

The Werewolf's Apprentice

"We book four guests per tour, you'll have to make up for the two empty seats."

"No problem." Leon handed her a Wachovia debit card.

"That will be twenty-four hundred, no refunds except for inclement weather, food and drinks included, since it's a private tour you can leave anytime you like. Captain Mike recommends no later than nine."

"Nine it is," said Samantha.

"Here's a sheet with the rules and terms. Captain Mike has the final say on everything while on the boat. I'm sure you understand, your safety is our highest priority."

Samantha stuffed it in her big straw bag.

Back in the car Leon pulled up the photo of the license.

"That's him all right, Mike Collins, Animal Control for the low country. He took out the Monks Corner colony. He disappeared after that." said Leon, "Didn't try too hard with the name. The picture's a match."

"He's mine, Leon. Don't you touch him."

"You sure he's your guy?"

"He's my guy. I don't have a picture of him. But I'm sure he was one of them, he worked Charleston undercover DEA, He knew my father. Bone told me. He wasn't supposed to."

"Take a look at this." Leon showed her the hunting photo. "That guy with the dogs? That's Decker. The Knoxville Animal Control guy. That's all you need to know."

"Small world," said Samantha. "This is getting personal. Not a good thing. Let's skip dinner I don't feel much like eating right now."

Samantha chewed the tip of her thumb as she watched the big shrimp boats tugging on their lines at the dock. The creaking of the lines and the smell of the marsh was still there, nothing had changed

.

"Tomorrow."

The Werewolf's Apprentice

The next day Leon and Samantha stepped out of the Benz into a steaming low country morning. Captain Mike was walking across the gravel parking lot with an orange Home Depot bucket sloshing with bait.

"Nice car," he said. "We don't see many of those around here."

"Thanks, we just got it," said Leon. "Not new, it's a lease return. Save a lot of money that way."

Samantha trailed along showing a lot of skin, swinging her big straw bag.

"We're all set to go. Climb on board."

The engines started, Mike moved the boat down Shem Creek running on points behind the other charter boats for the open Atlantic.

Samantha sat in the back smoking a Newport watching the shoreline recede.

The Werewolf's Apprentice

"So what are you looking for?" captain Mike asked. "The wahoo are running these days. We had good luck yesterday."

"Wahoo, by all means," Leon said. "How far out are they?"

"Gulf stream gets going thirty miles out, it's gonna take a while to get there. Food and drinks are in the cabin." He turned from the wheel and yelled to Samantha, "Please keep the smoking outside young lady."

She climbed up to where captain Mike stood behind the wheel.

"How long you been doing this, Mike?" She asked.

"I started when I was twelve years old. This was my dad's boat. I did some other stuff for a while, he died two years ago, I took over."

"Sorry, losing a parent is a special kind of pain," she said. "I'm an orphan myself."

"That's terrible, both parents?"

"Yes, they died in a boating accident. Their bodies were never recovered."

"When?"

"It was a long time ago, I was just a child. My uncle took me in, he was good to me, taught me everything I know. You have any kids?"

"Yes, a son, all grown up now, he's in the Army. My daughter graduates from University of South Carolina this spring. Top of her class in engineering of all things. Don't know where she got that from."

"I know you're proud of them, I'm sure they love you very much. Leon and I just got together, we're not ready to settle down just yet. We do a lot of traveling."

"What do you two do for a living?"

"We're rich."

"That's nice."

The boat droned on for another hour, the shoreline faded, soon only the spires of the Cooper River bridge were visible. Mike motioned to the GPS and on to the rougher water ahead. "Gulf Stream, see how the waves are running? It's going to get a bit rough, do you take seasick meds?"

"It takes a lot to make me sick."

The instrument panel went blank, the radio made a brief squawk and powered down.

"Shit, must be the breaker box again." Mike locked the wheel and dropped the engine speed to idle. "No problem, it happens. I'll be right back, we'll get out the lines and find you some fish."

Captain Mike entered the cabin, Leon was sitting at the galley table eating a Subway Turkey Supreme. "What's the matter?"

"Breaker tripped." Mike opened the panel. "I got it, right here." He ran his fingers down the panel of switches.

"That's funny."

"What's funny?" asked Leon.

"The breaker didn't trip, it's in the off position. Did you mess with this?"

"I don't know nothing about boats, Captain Mike. Ask Samantha, she's right over there."

Mike turned to see six feet of stark breathing werewolf standing between him and the open deck. He froze. He jumped and reached in a drawer for the flare gun he kept there. It was gone.

"You looking for this? Captain Mike Harmon." Leon said.

"Harmon? Who is he? I don't know anyone named Harmon. You got the wrong guy."

"You and your buddy, Decker, ever hunt more interesting game than boars?"

Harmon looked back and forth between Leon and Samantha.

"Who are you?" he asked.

Samantha closed the distance.

The Werewolf's Apprentice

"The last faces you will ever see," hissed Samantha.

Harmon backed up, he looked at Leon. Leon took a bite out of his Subway Turkey Supreme. "Subway is underrated don't you think, Samantha? This ain't half bad."

Samantha took another step.

"Please don't do this." Mike begged.

"Come on Captain Mike, get it all out. Admission of one's transgressions is the first step towards healing." Samantha said. "Right Leon?"

"I've always believed that." Leon was holding his cell in video mode. "Ever post dramatic footage on social Mike? Those people that hold it the wrong way, do you find that as annoying as I do?"

"Don't do this." Mike said.

"Sara Harper." Samantha said.

"Who is she?"

"John Harper's wife."

"I don't her either."

"That's funny, they were alive the day they took you out fishing."

Mike became strangely calm, "Who are you?" he asked again.

"Only at the point of dying." Samantha's blue gums parted revealing pearl white fangs still streaked red with blood from her shift.

Mike made a lunge for the door. Leon tripped him, he fell on his face against the wall of the cabin. Samantha jumped over him and smashed his head into the teak floor. She gently took his neck in her jaws and shook him.

"Wake up Captain Mike," Leon yelled from the table. "Show time."

Mike Harmon's eyes opened into the yellow eyes of Samantha glowing inches from his own.

"Meet Samantha Sarah Harper," said Leon. "She's the one that got away."

The Werewolf's Apprentice

Samantha tightened her grip, slowly crushing Mike's throat. Her fangs penetrated his skin, capillary blood began to seep. The taste burned in her mouth. She fought her wolf urge for more, she took her time. Samantha held him so, listening to his desperate breathing. His eyes turned glassy. She closed deeper cutting into his muscle and bone, his spine snapped under her jaws, he relaxed in her grip.

"He didn't fight much," said Leon.

She dropped him dead on the floor. "Must be a fish knife around here somewhere, Leon take care of this one please. I'll turn us around."

The next morning Captain Courageous was found rocking sideways in the surf off Station thirty-two on Sullivan's Island. No body was recovered, the police did note signs of struggle. Only one piece of evidence was recovered. A subway bag containing a human ear, removed with surgical precision, a lipstick stained one-dollar bill and a rather small capacity USB drive. Attempts to locate his wife, Amanda Collins were unsuccessful as well as their attempts to find any records regarding the last charter she booked.

Back in Virginia Jake stared at the two packages on his desk. One, a resignation letter.

"I'm gone. Don't try to find me, I wiped everything. You should do the same. Best, Truett."

The second contained a Subway bag and its contents. Jake already watched the video in the crime lab. The sight of two werewolves feeding on Harmon shook him to his core. He never had truly acknowledged that reality. He looked out his window across a perfect lawn to the woods beyond.

Closer.

Jake opened his secure phone and called a number in Yugoslavia. The phone rang through the hiss of copper wires strung up a castle wall in the damp mountains outside Belgrade.

"Franz Salozar, to whom do I have the pleasure of speaking? ...Ahh Jake, so good to hear from you. Wolf troubles again?"

I-95

Leon and Samantha abandoned the Mercedes in student parking at Columbia College out on North Main in Columbia. They walked along perfect sidewalks past perfect buildings. At the main entrance they stopped for a white Honda hung with DEBEE vanity tags, driven by a somewhat harried lady rushing through the gate.

"Nice place," Samantha said.

A few blocks down the street began the usual line of used car lots. Rows of high mileage cars sat under flag pennants with "look at me" stickers on the windshields. Leon walked along the broken sidewalk looking for an inconspicuous General Motors product. He settled on a fat toad of a Buick Regal with a Clemson sticker on the rear window and greasy cloth seats that smelled like French fries. A half our later they hit the north bound 95 just outside Irmo.

The Werewolf's Apprentice

"Another one, I'm getting tired of this," Leon said.

Samantha held him. She kissed his lips. "It's almost done. We don't have to go back to Faith after this. Hell, there may not be anyone there anyway. We can find a place and make our lives what we want."

"Jake and Dog are the only ones left. They'll be ready for us this time," he said.

"I know."

*****

Dog walked out of the mine shaft into the bright sunshine. Before him the ghost town of Bodie, California. Paranormal Productions trucks were everywhere. A detail of men fitted out like an Iraq Blackwater hit squad followed him to the pyro truck.

An older man with steel blue eyes in a denim jacket wearing unlaced tennis shoes was waiting. The man handed Dog a clipboard.

The Werewolf's Apprentice

"Dirty Harry model 357 magnum, blank loads, serial 12376. Please sign here."

Dog took the weapon and strapped the holster on his waist.

"Heavy," he said.

"Biggest baddest revolver on the planet," the prop manager said. "You got a bit of history in your hand Dog, this is the actual prop used by Eastwood in the Dirty Harry movies."

"That's good luck. Maybe we'll make some Eastwood money on this show," Dog smiled, he rested his hand on the gun at his side.

"You know the rules, keep the gun on you at all times, nobody touches it except you. Bring it back to me personally, only you can sign it back in."

"Got it," said Dog, "No problem."

Dog walked up to the entrance of the mine followed by the security men and the camera crew.

The Werewolf's Apprentice

The prop man locked the door to the van and left in a white Camry parked a short distance away.

Twenty minutes later Dog lifted the 357, yelled "Stop asshole," in dramatic fashion and pulled the trigger. The hammer came down on the large cartridge spiking the primer. Rather than igniting a black powder flash blank, the primer ignited a charge of plastic explosive one thousand times more powerful. The gun disintegrated into stainless steel shards, slicing off two of Dog's fingers and taking a chunk of meat from his ear. The hammer, freed from its casing, cut through the bullet proof vest and lodged in his sternum.

*****

The fat Buick four door sedan waddled at highway speeds up I-95 past Pedro's South of the Border into North Carolina. Leon was carving a heart in the fake wood on the dash with Samantha's nail file. "You think it's ok to use our real initials?"

"Like that, Yoda would not."

Leon's cell buzzed. "Message from the high command," he said.

"What now?"

"It's from Bone."

"And?"

"Dog hit failed, only wounded."

"Now we're in the shit," Samantha said. "We're never going to get another chance at him."

"There's more." Leon said.

"All targets are on the move, keep low until we contact you with instructions."

"The uncles are getting nervous. Don't want the kids to mess up." Samantha said.

"Full moon tonight my love." Leon said.

The Werewolf's Apprentice

Wallops Island

"It's getting late, I'm tired of driving," said Samantha, "Over there, the Astro Inn, gateway to Wallops Island. *Ice Cold Air Conditioning in Every Room Cool Your Jets Here.*"

Samantha traded the shower with Leon and cranked the AC control into the blue. Her silver ear studs had begun to warm with the oncoming rising moon. She removed them and placed them in the ash tray by the bed.

Leon came out of the shower, naked and steaming wet to behold Samantha fully shifted in front of him. Her shimmering fur caught the moon, the silver alpha streak on her back glowed in the soft light. Her animal smell filled the room. Leon removed his studs and shifted before her into a full young alpha male, energy surged through his every vein. He crawled up her and took the back of her neck in his ivory teeth. His tender bite unlocked all the heat she had to give.

They joined on the floor as the first light of the moon flowed through the clouds. Unburdened by any trace of humanity they tore the room to shreds until the moon set in the west.

They lay there together in the ruins of their bed. "No loving like wolf loving," said Leon.

"We've been lucky," said Samantha.

Samantha put her arm on Leon's warm chest, she felt his heart. "What about that unfinished business of yours in Knoxville? We're close."

"I've been thinking about that."

"I thought getting that guy in Mount Pleasant would change things," she said, "I'm still the same."

"I won't let it go," said Leon. "I'm not looking for peace, I'm looking for revenge. Same as you."

The Werewolf's Apprentice

She pulled her long red nails across his chest leaving rough streaks in his skin. "I've been thinking about that. We're the endpoint of a long game. Selected and raised from childhood for this day. Yoda and Bone must be hundreds of years old, they know about time. It's no wonder we're together in this room tonight."

Leon took a deep breath, "You and I do the work of soldiers, but that's not what we're about. We have a right to be happy. And we will, when the work is done."

"What if they ask for more?" Samantha said.

Two children ran past their door laughing. Samantha and Leon stared at the ceiling together in silence.

Samantha walked naked into the shower. Leon lay in a perfect moment watching her form moving behind the steaming glass.

The Werewolf's Apprentice

Knoxville

They dumped the Buick in Murfreesboro. They bought a Craig's List Honda Odyssey Lx minivan with six months left on the tags at a trailer park just outside the city limits.

"I miss that Benz 500," said Samantha, she stubbed her Newport out on the dash, "This thing smells like chickens."

"It's not far to Knoxville, we get this done, I'll buy you something real nice."

"I'm gonna start wearing dresses from now on."

"What brought this on?"

"Don't know, just feel like it. I'm feeling more feminine these days."

"What will we be doing when we don't do this anymore? Yoda may want us to start flying again."

"I don't want to go back to Faith," she said.

"Me neither."

"Key West sounds nice. I like the Caribbean."

The Werewolf's Apprentice

"No woods down there."

"Screw the woods, I'm getting too old for that. I break my nails when I shift. We've done our bit. I want a normal life, whatever that is."

"People who wear silver studs in their ears every full moon don't get to play at normal," said Leon.

Samantha leaned close and took Leon's ear in her teeth. She bit down and shook her head gently, nibbling Leon's ear lobe with her tongue. "I don't wanna give up *everything*."

"You quit that right now, it makes my nose itch, here comes the big bridge. Which exit do we take?"

They checked into a long-term executive housing suite on the better side of Knoxville. The next day they went out and bought a silver Nissan Sentra and two white Camrys to replace the minivan. Late that afternoon Leon waited in one of the Camrys watching the Knoxville police station talking by cell to Samantha in the Sentra. Two unmarked Ford

Escape police specials were lined up in the station reserved area.

"He's careful," said Leon, "No hits on an address or anything. Guess the cops have their reasons."

"Here comes someone," she said.

"Not him."

Five minutes later Daniel Patrick walked out the door. He paused on the steps talking to a large red-faced man holding a lawyer's satchel.

"That's him. Sam you take the first leg, I'll follow your GPS."

The Escape rolled easy down Main and picked up the interstate leading out of town. They followed Patrick past exits for car malls and shopping centers, a few miles out he turned onto a secondary road.

"Switch time," said Leon, "Follow me."

Now Leon held the Escape in his eyes. Patrick drove through an electric gate leading to sprawling brick ranch sitting in a third of an acre of perfect lawn. Two beagles ran out to meet him. Leon dropped a map pin on the GPS and kept moving.

"Sam, do a turnaround in his driveway, see if you catch anything. I'll meet you back at the suite."

"I'm there now, he's petting the dogs."

The next day was a Tuesday. It was eleven thirty, Samantha and Leon were sitting together in the Camry outside city hall. Patrick and three guys walked out and got in the car.

"Here he comes, looks like detectives with him, same car, same spot."

"Ok, nice and easy," Samantha moved out into traffic two cars behind.

"Lunch run with the boys," Leon said."

"I could do with a little lunch myself," said Samantha.

"Are you out of your mind?"

The Werewolf's Apprentice

"They don't know me from Saul of Tarsus Leon, I'll just walk in and sit down. Maybe I can hear something with my wolfie ears."

"This is a real bad idea."

"No Leon, this is an opportunity, it's worth the risk."

Leon looked nervous, "I'm going in too, separate table."

The Escape stopped in a gravel parking lot outside a log cabin of a building signed Gumlog's BBQ. Leon dropped Samantha off on the street and went in and parked.

The interior of Gumlog's smelled of pork. People sat in lines on varnished pine benches under the smiling faces of prize hogs decorated with farm show medallions and pictures of high school baseball teams. Patrick and his friends were called past the line by the hostess and taken directly to the dining room.

Leon sized up the menu, Samantha sat across from him playing some pegboard game. The door opened, in walked a face that Leon would never forget, Jim Decker, the dog man. He went to the hostess who walked him to Patrick's table. Leon caught Samantha's eye and nodded his head at the man. Samantha paid no apparent attention, they called her name next. Leon put down his menu and left.

She returned a half hour later carrying a take-out box full of meat.

"You should see those people eat in there. Those people are huge. Gumlog is the Hajj of Hog. A temple to the swine," she said. "I got us four *Full Hog* plates, two racks of ribs and a pecan pie."

Samantha pulled out a rib, stripped it clean with one stroke and tossed it out the window. "Fortune favors the bold my love. Bone would be right proud of us now."

"What did they say?"

"Decker yapped about his dogs the whole time. He talked about this hunting place called *The Bat Farm.*

Sounded like they go there a lot. Said they are all going out there for some kind of hunting thing."

"That's where he keeps his dogs." said Leon. "Deep woods, good location for us, we need to find that place."

"We gotta get them both," Samantha said, "if we screw up on one the other will run. We'll never find him."

"Dog used to work for Decker. Maybe he'll show up too."

"Nobody gets that lucky Leon."

Leon waved at the cars in the lot, "Which one of those cars out there is Decker's?"

"I'm betting on the camo four-wheel drive Suburban with the dog cage in the back."

"I'm gonna tag it."

Leon and Samantha sat low in the car waiting for the men to leave. Decker came out first, the men stood talking for a while, Decker got in the Suburban and drove away.

"Got him. Let's go back to the place, those ribs are driving me nuts."

They lay on the bed in the hotel watching the GPS signal from Decker's truck sitting in town near the police station.

"It's getting late, he should be moving soon," said Leon.

"Email from Bone," Samantha said, "they got a hit on Dog at the Nashville airport."

"I told you, he's coming here, I know it. Where else would he go?"

"That's three," said Samantha.

"That leaves Jake and Truett," said Leon. "Unless they show up too."

"Nobody gets that lucky Leon."

"My dad used to tell me one day I'd get lucky."

"He was talking you meeting me Leon. This is something else entirely."

The Werewolf's Apprentice

"Bone said Truett's gone dark."

"He'll show up eventually," Leon pointed to the screen. "There, Decker's moving."

* * * * *

Five men walked down the concourse of the Knoxville airport. Four were in casual attire sporting Euro haircuts and tiny vestigial beards. They were big men, they walked in a strong loping fashion. The only indication that they might be true blood werewolves was the lack of buttons on their shirts and loose slip-on shoes. Leading the way, an aloof, pale man of some breeding holding a silver topped cane. He wore a satin cape with red lining that flowed behind him in an aura of strangeness. The locals turned their heads as the crew passed the coffee and snack shops on their way to the baggage claim. He seemed to like the attention. He was met at the baggage claim by a fifth werewolf with silver studs in his ears. Minutes later they entered a black stretch limo and headed for town.

* * * * *

"He's stopped," said Samantha. "Here's the satellite."

"Nice place, big cabin, a barn or dog kennel, lake. Middle of nowhere," said Leon.

"*The Bat Farm,* perfect.*"* Samantha was biting her thumb again. She lit a Newport. "Look, there's even a dirt road off the highway to the lake. We'll use that. They might have cameras and shit on the main entrance."

"This is a no smoking-room Sam, we're gonna get charged."

"We're talking about taking down two, maybe three Animal Control guys in one swoop and you're crawling up my ass for that?"

Leon snatched the cigarette from Samantha's mouth. In that case, I'll take this one."

The Werewolf's Apprentice

"Ohh, grumpy, are you? Wolfman, patience you must learn," Samantha slapped Leon on the butt and lit a fresh one.

"Let's watch, as soon as he leaves we go take a look at the place," said Leon.

"I'll ping Bone, maybe he has a Dog update." Samantha banged out an email.

"Switch over to Patrick, where is he now?" said Leon.

"He just got home."

"Tomorrow will be perfect. One hundred percent moon. We can go full-up alpha on their asses." said Samantha. "All we need is the Dog. Where is the Dog?"

Three hours passed, to two AM.

Samantha came out of the shower wearing nothing but a huge t-shirt with a big yellow duck on the back. Leon was half asleep at the screen. "Patrick's in for the night," he said. "Decker is still out there. I'll set the tracking alarm, let's go to bed."

The Werewolf's Apprentice

Morning, Samantha and Leon were eating bacon at the local waffle place.

"Decker went to the grocery this morning, went straight to the *Bat Farm*. That's it," said Samantha.

"Bone say anything about Dog?"

"Dog is MIA."

Leon finished off the bacon, "Let's go to Gumlog again, load up the cooler with the meaty meat, we're gonna be busy tonight. We'll need that meat when we're done."

"We play it cool," said Samantha, "We have time on our side. We go in, sneak around, if we get an opportunity we jump them. Use the 357 on them, silver bullets are as good as lead on a human. Dead is dead. Nobody said we have to do it wolf style."

"Except for Decker," said Leon, "He gets it the hard way."

"Don't screw around. Don't make it personal."

The Werewolf's Apprentice

"That boat captain in Charleston? You sure took your time with him."

"This is different, Captain Mike was alone, we were two on one, you didn't even put down your sandwich. We don't know what we're gonna find out there. Use the gun, you can eat them later if you want."

"That's not the same thing and you know it," said Leon.

The Bat Farm

They left the Nissan at the boat landing at the end of the road and started into the woods towards the farm. Leon carried the 357 in a canvas pouch draped over his neck.

They threaded their way out of the brush by the lake into a stand of long needle pines, dusk fell, the full moon was still an hour to rise, the silver studs in their ears began warming, holding back the beast inside.

Leon took a reading on his phone.

"This way, we need to avoid that barn or kennel, whatever it is. Don't want to wake the hounds."

Minutes later they were at the back of the hunting lodge. The fireplace was roaring.

"There's Decker and Patrick," said Leon.

"Here comes another," said Samantha, "Oh this is sweet, it's Dog. See the hand? Bone did that."

"That's a lot of food, they're expecting guests."

The Werewolf's Apprentice

"Here comes a car," Samantha said. "Get down."

A big Lincoln stretch limousine rolled up to the lodge. The doors opened, they heard the crunching of shoes on the gravel. Decker got up and opened the door. A man wearing a cape came in followed by five men. It was Franz Salozar, freshly arrived from Belgrade with his Euro wolf companions.

"Trouble. Six more," said Leon.

"That guy in the cape, he's an old world blood sucker if I ever saw one," said Samantha.

"Those other guys look like true bloods. Big ones. Look, they're beginning to shift, moon's got them, they can't help it."

"Five true bloods, we're screwed. No way we can handle this."

Cries of pain and dogs howling came from the barn. The men pulled rifles off the moose head over the fireplace and left the lodge.

The Werewolf's Apprentice

"Closer," Leon moved down a low ditch across from the barn.

The men slid open the rolling doors. The howling rolled out into the night. Inside were two rows of barred enclosures. On one side Decker's dogs danced and barked with joy. On the other side werewolves paced at the bars shifting and howling with hate in their yellow eyes. Decker came out with his dogs. They gathered around him as the father of all things good. He attached leashes and stood next to the limo feeding them treats from a bag.

"My God they must have ten shifters locked up in those cages," whispered Leon. "What for?"

"We're gonna find out soon," said Samantha.

Patrick pulled a remote control from his pocket.

"What do you have in there?" asked Franz.

"Shifters, domestics. Sometimes we get lucky and trank one with a dart. We keep them here for the dogs, a lot more fun than chasing racoons."

The Werewolf's Apprentice

"Stand back boys, let's run down a wolfie." The remote flickered red in his hand. From inside came the clank and squeal of a cage door opening on rusty hinges. The men stood there waiting. Nothing happened.

"Why doesn't he come out?" asked Franz.

"Would you?" said Patrick. "Hey Decker, send one of your boys in there to after him."

Decker unleased the large German Shepherd. The animal sat at attention waiting, watching Decker's every move. Decker went to his knee, almost cheek to cheek. He spoke softly, "action"

The dog ran into the barn. The sounds of a struggle echoed inside, a long cry of pain, then silence.

The dog's head flew out the door and rolled up to Decker's feet.

"That's quite enough. That son of a bitch killed my best dog. Let's get him."

The Werewolf's Apprentice

The men approached the doors shining lights inside. The lamps illuminated unmistakable black form of a werewolf, a seven-foot beast with glowing yellow eyes standing over the headless corpse of the dog. He smashed through a window and tore out into the forest.

Decker unleashed the rest of his animals. Franz called to his pack, his Euro true bloods had fully shifted by now. They took off running with the hounds, they were fast, Dog the bounty hunter followed close, Decker and Patrick took up the rear. Franz sauntered into the barn alone sniffing the air.

"You know anything about vampires?" said Leon, "I've never seen one before."

"I read *Queen of the Damned* few years back, that's about it," said Samantha. "I guess if you tear off enough parts they'll die like anything else."

The Werewolf's Apprentice

Leon hid the gun under a feed sack and shifted. "Let's go get him. I'll go in first, he might think I'm one of the others. You come as soon as I hit him."

Samantha shifted. She was pacing back and forth; her eyes were gleaming. Her golden wolf necklace glinted in the moonlight.

Leon trotted into the barn. Franz was standing at a cage raking his cane against the bars. All along the wall nine fully shifted werewolves stared back. Leon squatted next to him.

"Why are you not running with the pack?" he said in Yugoslavian.

Leon flea scratched the back of his ear.

"I need no one to guard me, that is quite unnecessary. Back to the hunt with you."

With that Leon lunged at the outline of the vampire's arm under the cape. The first taste of ancient blood surged through Leon like sparks from a power line. Franz tried to pull away but Leon's jaws were locked to him, he felt the bones cracking under his jaws. Franz twisted the wolf head top of his cane. A silver dagger sprang into his hand. The top of the cane sprouted a crown of silver spikes. Franz drove the dagger into Leon's neck. Burning pain radiated throughout Leon's body, he held on. Samantha came in at full strength. Franz spun the cane into the side of her head, he pulled away chunks of blood soaked fur. She fell. Franz turned his weapon again to Leon, smashing the length of his body with the poison spikes. Leon rolled away under the blows leaving a trail of blood in the straw floor. Franz threw off the cape revealing his ruffled red soaked shirt with pearl buttons. "Now you die wolf boy." He raised the spiked cane to strike.

Samantha gathered herself and lunged for Franz's leg. She caught him just above the ankle, she bit down with all her strength. The cracking of ancient bones and the first taste of his blood roared in her head. She found the ropy

Achilles tendon and ripped it up and out the back of his calf. The damage done, she released and positioned for another strike. She saw the first evidence of pain as Franz's foot hit the packed earth and twisted back at a grotesque angle against his torn calf. Still he moved to her, steady and calm, his fangs rose.

Samantha turned on her Garou charm, a blue wave of energy bloomed and engulfed Franz. He stopped advancing, a curious look came over him. "How very interesting, so long since I've faced the Garou, I was wondering why it was so hard breaking you."

Samantha backed away, low and breathing hard. She drew him deeper into the barn away from Leon. Leon struggled, crawling towards a set of handles on the wall. She felt herself growing weaker. Franz advanced. She projected charm once again.

"You're fading," Franz gleamed, "I can feel it. Your powers are of no effect against my kind. Nobody told you that? Now I take the blood of the Loup-Garou, a rare and marvelous thing."

Franz leap eight feet in the air and came down at Samantha holding his dagger in both hands. His dagger whistled in her face, it found bone cutting a splitting sharp line in her forehead. Blood flowed into her eyes.

Leon crawled over and up against the far wall. He fumbled with the cage release above him with his twisted paws. It didn't yield.

Franz kept coming, hobbling. Samantha retreated time and time again from the whistling blade, further and further into the barn. Franz caught her in a stumble, he ripped a deep gash in her leg with the dagger, the pain was exquisite, her flesh bloomed red. She tried to stand but fell back. Franz smiled, he raised his bright curved ivory fangs. He began to hammer Samantha with his cane, driving the silver spikes into her body over and over again.

The Werewolf's Apprentice

Leon struggled higher and took the release it in his jaws and fell. The stress on his wound seared white hot into his neck and shoulders. Behind him came the sound of cages opening.

The shifted prisoners swarmed the vampire, expending their full measure of hate upon him. He swung wildly at his attackers as they fell over each other howling for his flesh. He struggled, he was strong, he died hard, the persistent ripping of meat from bone eventually took its price. He was torn into quivering lumps of undead scattered in pieces on the ground. A werewolf twisted in death in the straw with the sliver blade in his chest. Two wolves fought over the remains of Franz's head peeling the skin from his face like a latex mask.

Leon ran to his precious Samantha. He found her laying in a pile of bags, bleeding from the deep cut in her front leg and the savage wounds from the cane. She looked into Leon's eyes and drew strength from him. She threw off her pain, rose up and shifted against the moon through sheer force of will. She took silver studs and pressed them into Leon's bloody ears. As he recovered, the healing power of the Lycan rebuilt his wounded neck, the pain receded, and he stood. The remaining werewolves gathered around them panting. They stirred for a moment, communicating at a level no human could ever understand. They became of one mind and took off to the woods.

Leon retrieved his gun bag and stumbled with his mate to the lodge. They gobbled down the remains of the feast left behind. Restored and healed, but unable to afford another shift, they went to the woods.

Lust for revenge focused the minds of the avenging pack released from the barn. They found the trail to their prey easy. The Euros had run ahead with Dog, leaving Patrick and Decker far behind. The Euro pack had split up to block and surround their tiring victim. The wolves from the barn hunted as one in a pack, they isolated and attacked each Euro in turn. One by one they fell.

Decker and Patrick stood alone in the dark forest listening to the sounds of the struggle. The cries rose and faded as each Euro wolf fell. Across the woods came the pathetic yelping of Decker's hounds as they were run down and consumed. The pack found Dog. Decker and Patrick stood with mouths open at the inhuman cries of Dog as the pack took him apart. Decker and Patrick began running through the brush. At the end of the trail with the lodge in sight they froze. Samantha's finely muscled body stood gleaming blue and naked in the moonlight before them.

"Who the fuck are you?" said Decker.

He felt the heartless barrel of an ancient 357 magnum against his skull.

"Don't move Decker."

Leon took Decker's pearl handled revolver and handed it to Samantha. They faced the men with flickering yellow eyes on the edge of the shift. Leon's hands ached as he suppressed the urge to form claws.

"Who are you?" Patrick barely formed the words.

"Damonia Estrella."

"Who is that? Never heard of her."

"Mitch Goldman."

The first flickers of memory turned Decker's face into a portrait of fear.

"Billy Estrella, he was my brother."

Decker found the answer. "It's you. Knoxville, the boy."

"Yes I am. And I'm here because of what you did."

Leon raised the heavy revolver, the moon glinted off the barrel.

"And this is my father's gun."

Two shots echoed through the forest. Two men fell dead into the rotting leaves.

Leon kicked dirt onto their faces.

Leon and Samantha retrieved their clothes and took the vampire's cape as a trophy for Bone. They returned to the lodge.

The Feast

In the kitchen they found a twenty pound turkey browning in the oven along with a large ham.

"Well lookee here," said Leon, "How nice."

Samantha ripped out a chunk of turkey breast with her bare hands. "Let's get to work."

A half hour later they sat at the rough table surrounded by the remains. Leon ran his fingers over the fading scars from Franz's spiked cane. "That guy was tough."

"They die hard," she said. "Now it's Jake time. He'll go down easy."

Leon put his gun on the table, "Enough."

"What did you say?"

"We're done."

"We're not done." she said.

The Werewolf's Apprentice

Leon took a deep breath and blew it out at the ceiling. He dug in his heels. "Wasn't this enough? That guy had us in there. That vampire is not the only one, more will come. Sooner or later they'll get us. There's nobody left but Jake. He knows he's next. He'll bring a whole frigging vampire army down on us."

Samantha coiled, "So, this is it. You get what you want. Now you're going to quit."

"You know Yoda has a 'B' team to cover things if we get nailed. Let them wrap things up," he said.

Samantha oozed contempt. Leon felt her heat across the room.

"Who saved your baby wolf pup ass from being torn to pieces by Decker's dogs in Knoxville? Are you that ungrateful? We owe a debt to Bone and that debt will be paid in full. I'll finish this, alone if I have to."

"Look at us. Does anything bother you anymore? We're becoming less than human every day," said Leon. "We're getting weaker, the wolf in us gets stronger every time, if we keep going what will become of us?"

"There will be no rest, we keep going until we run the last one down, until we've made an end to them." Leon felt Samantha's will coming on to him.

"We've been out so long, we're lost," said Leon, "Once I was sure we could find our way back to what we were that night in Wisconsin. Now I'm not so sure."

Samantha cooled, "We carry the other inside us, but we are not monsters."

Samantha reached out to him, she touched him, the force of her love overwhelmed him, her animal charm filled the room. She opened a channel no human could ever comprehend. She entered his mind.

"I don't want anything more than to be with you. Wolf or human, I don't care, if we're together that's enough for me."

Leon lifted the gun from the table. "Let's go."

208

The Werewolf's Apprentice

The gate buzzer rang.

"It never ends. Who the hell can this be?" he said.

He looked at the gate monitor, a gaunt fifty-five-year-old face in need of a shave stared at the camera with sunken eyes drawn over with worry.

"Yes?" Leon asked.

"It's me, Jake, I'm late. Let me in."

"Now we have him," Samantha said.

Leon pressed the gate release. He wrapped the vampire cape around his shoulders and sat in the big chair by the fire. Samantha's eyes were glowing with blood hunger. Leon raised the dead vampire's cane. "Easy now Sam, first he must confess, I want to hear it."

She gathered up the serving tray and ran to the kitchen.

Moments later, a government issue Ford rumbled up to the door and stopped by the Limo.

"Come in," said Leon.

Jake entered, he looked nervously around the room. He looked uncomfortable.

Leon rose to greet him. "Franz Salozar at your service." He bowed.

Jake seemed relieved, "All these years I've never seen your face. Franz, here you are in person at last. You look much younger than I imagined."

"Ahh, invisible to mirrors, invisible to the web, nothing really changes does it?" said Leon. He tapped dead Franz's cane on the floor. "Please sit. Care for a little something to eat? A glass of wine perhaps?"

"Sabri, bring us some refreshments please."

Samantha walked in from the kitchen with a bottle and a platter. She placed them on the table, uncorked the bottle and poured a glass. For a hanging moment Jake wondered what sex would be like with the Sabri the vampire. She noticed his veiled snake eye flirtation as she sat down, she gave him a wisp of encouragement.

"Sorry we can't join you," said Leon, "Sabri and I have dietary restrictions you know."

Jake downed a turkey drumstick and emptied his glass. Samantha refilled it. "Where is everyone?"

"Out with the dogs, running down a rather unfortunate werewolf," Leon laughed. "What sport, like the fox hunts back home. I've never seen anything so exciting."

"I don't know why those guys keep those devils alive. One day one of them is gonna get loose and make a mess."

"Seems harmless enough," said Leon.

"I wanna kill them all. Too bad those assholes got the Moose," said Jake, "We were setting up the lab again. Moose was working on an Ebola hybrid targeted for shifters. A bit more time and we could have plagued every one of them out of existence, every frigging one of them."

"We might have some objections to that," Leon said. "We've reached an accommodation with our werewolves, they can be quite useful."

"Bullshit, they're all the same Franz, they'll turn on you. They're brutal, dumb animals, they don't think like you and me."

"If your little germ toy gets loose in Europe your life will be an unnaturally short one. I'd be very upset if I lost my little friends."

"Enough of this dancing around. Did you find those two? That's what I paid you for."

"Oh yes, we never fail. As a matter of fact, they are right here. Waiting your pleasure."

Jake saw Samantha flash her yellow wolf eyes across the table.

"What is this?"

Leon reached to a platter covered with a chrome plated dome. "Some dessert, perhaps?"

Leon lifted the cover to reveal two severed ears laying on a lettuce bed of dollar bills with Samantha's red kisses on them.

The Werewolf's Apprentice

"I'm not sure which is which, but those would be Patrick and Decker, as for the Dog, he's wolf shit by now."

Leon rang the plate with a tap of his fork, "We seem to be missing an ear."

"You're the ones." said Jake, "You're them."

Jake shifted and started rising from his chair. Leon produced the gun.

"Sit down, we've wanted to meet you for such a long time. Share a few more moments with Samantha and me."

"What do you want?"

"Only one thing."

With that, Samantha burned her charm into the center of Jake's brain. His head froze rigid as his back seized into a mass of constricted muscle.

Samantha and Leon said no more. She duct taped Jake into his chair. They poured kerosene from the wall heater in a circle around Jake and up to the edge of the fireplace. Samantha turned him to the face the flames. She took a strip of duct tape and stuck Jake's eyelids wide open to his forehead.

Leon poked Jake with the cane, "Ain't that Samantha something? You still with us?"

Samantha leaned into Jake's face, his eyes followed hers, twitching, he moved his mouth, but no words came out. Samantha soaked the cape in the fuel and draped it around Jake's shoulders.

"I have something for you."

She kissed him full on the mouth with her flaming red lips.

Leon poured the remainder of the kerosene up and into the fireplace. A thin line of blue flame flared and ran down igniting the circle around the chair. She released Jake from the charm, he began to struggle.

They stood outside watching the lodge burn listening to the screams.

"We better get going," said Samantha.

"Game over," Leon said.

Samantha jingled the keys to the limo. "Not quite, something's come up. There is another, just one more. Please don't get upset with me, I'll do this one all by myself."

The Werewolf's Apprentice

Truett

Truett backed out of his garage in Bellingham, Washington. On the seat next to him a messenger bag filled with term papers from his eleventh-grade civics class. It was damp outside. The wipers popped every two seconds scraping the drizzle off the windshield. Truett's big issue this morning was an annoying streak left by a twig trapped under the driver's side blade.

Truett was a man of minor persistent habits. He still used the same ATM code from ten years ago. The same went for passwords. *DogBreath1999* was scattered across a few hundred web sites over the last twenty years. He thought nothing of using it when he signed up on a dating site last month. Truett was a man at peace, confident he had completely wiped his digital footprint that last day in Virginia. He felt comfortable and secure in his new skin as a Master of Political Science from Purdue.

The Werewolf's Apprentice

But in the cloud a tag is a tag and tags are forever. Somewhere out on the dark web a tireless bot determined the unique and very strong password that popped up in Bellingham was a one in one billion match to a certain person of interest, a person who went dark in Virginia over a year ago.

Truett waited his turn, as he did every weekday morning, in a drive through a few blocks from school. He paid no attention to the rather attractive woman that handed him his sausage biscuit. If he had, he might have noticed a wolf's head on a blue silk ribbon around her neck.

He parked in the faculty section at Bellingham High and opened the bag. Finals are next week, summer break is within reach. He took a bite. A cyanide loaded gel cap split between his teeth.

Funny, this smells like almonds.

The End

The Werewolf's Apprentice

The Werewolf's Apprentice was written in a rather small house surrounded by feral cats. I hope you enjoyed it.

Find other works by Mike here.

www.venicecreative.com

The Werewolf's Apprentice

What do you say when a beautiful woman shows up at your office with a bag of money and asks if you are interested stealing five hundred pounds of radioactive stones from a Nevada Test Site? When she looks like Damonia Estrella, the answer is 'when do we leave?'

What do you do when this beautiful woman turns out to be a werewolf, and steps out of a shower in a silk bathrobe saying she wants to 'get to know you better'?

These are the problems of Mitch Goldman, paranormal investigator. He's not entirely in control of the situation but he's not sure he wants out just yet.

The Werewolf's Apprentice

California Cougars can be shapeshifters too. Kim meets a guy that shares her love of wildlife photography. But she has no idea just how much more he shares with the wildlife he is so interested in protecting. And there is his 'cousin' from Charleston, Sabbath who seems to disappear at the strangest times.

The Werewolf's Apprentice

Soper's Hole, Tortola, British Virgin Islands, Karen and Amanda, the owners of the dive boat Marshall Tucker are facing ruin. A client, Kurt, arrives looking to hire a boat to take him to the island of Anegada. Dive tours to the shallow reefs of the island are off limits, the outer reaches of Horseshoe reef hold the ruins of ships all the way back to the 1400's. It's a bit of a risk and the guy with the money is just what Karen is looking for. But the baggage includes the mysterious Robin, a woman with scars from bullets who shares a past with Kurt that is not open for discussion.

The Werewolf's Apprentice

A coffee shop romance gets complicated. Sylvia is finally scraping her old boyfriend off the bottom of her shoe. Before she's done here comes John. He's too good to be true and as it turns out he is. Things get deep fast, John's 'partner' Robin arrives. She's not competition for Sylvia, she's muscle for John's next operation. Sylvia keeps swimming towards the deep end, finally she finds out that John and Robin are on a mission to save the world. That's more than she expected.

The Werewolf's Apprentice

A quiet North Georgia Lake Town, surrounded by fences, put in place to protect the residents. But nobody knows just what from. Justin Meriwether rides his bike along the fence every week, this week he sees a woman, Rachel, sitting in a lawn chair with a stopwatch and a map timing lighting strikes out of the approaching storm. She has a plan and Justin is the last piece of the puzzle.

Made in the USA
Coppell, TX
06 April 2022

76147784R00125